# MURDER IN BLACK AND WHITE

### N. L. Quatrano

## Book 1: The Point and Shoot Mystery Series

Print ISBN-13: 978-0-9854381-0-4
Also available in Kindle and eBook formats

Copyright © 2015 Nancy L. Quatrano
Cover design by Rik Feeney of PublishingSuccessOnline.com
Cover images used by license from Dreamstime
@photoeuphoria/Dreamstime.com
@bartekwardziak/Dreamstime.com

Printed in the United States of America

*WC Publishing*
an On-Target Words company™
147 Patriot Lane
Elkton, FL 32145 USA
www.WCPublish.com

# What people are saying…

"N. L. Quatrano writes a classic 'whodunit' with an edgy heroine, quirky characters, and an intricate plot that will keep the reader turning the pages into the wee hours!"
- Jan Coffey, author of TROPICAL KISS

"MURDER IN BLACK AND WHITE by N. L. Quatrano is one of those rare books that I simply couldn't put down. Every time I thought I had it figured out, I'd get blindsided by yet another twist I hadn't seen coming. Great dialog, a setting so well described I felt like I'd been there before and characters who were easy to get to know and care about. Please tell me there's a sequel. I'm looking forward to more adventures with Antonia and Travis."
- Skye Taylor, author of WHATEVER IT TAKES and the series, The Camerons of Tides Way

In N.L. Quatrano's mystery thriller, Murder in Black and White, the town of Chastity Creek is taken by storm when a woman is unexpectedly murdered. When private detective AJ Buchanan stumbles upon the dead body of her best friend's mother, she is recruited to help find the person responsible for the crime and bring them to justice. However, what starts out as a normal murder investigation turns out to be more complicated than expected, and sucks AJ into a world of hidden family secrets, vengeance, and guilt. Fans of powerful female characters will enjoy this book as the protagonist, AJ, is strong, intelligent and will stop at nothing to unravel the murder of Matilda Renkin. The plot is fast-paced, engaging and suspenseful. When readers think they know what's about to happen, Quatrano throws in a surprise twist that will leave readers wanting more more. In addition, Quatrano's expertly crafted descriptions and world building are spectacular; readers will feel as though they are in Chastity Creek, experiencing the small town and its unique characters. A classic whodunit story with plenty of suspense and drama, Murder in Black and White is a thoroughly entertaining page turner that will keep readers on the edge of their seats! – Review by the Book Excellence Awards

## By Marie Vernon, St. Augustine Record

Posted Oct 24, 2015 at 3:05 PM

When Antonia Buchanan agrees to help town matriarch Matilda Rankin compile her family history, she little suspects that she's signing on for a dangerous project. That realization comes quickly when Antonia enters the old paper mill once owned by the Rankin family and discovers Matilda's dead body. It is murder or a natural death? That's the first question Antonia and the authorities must determine.

Antonia thinks it's murder, especially when an emailed poem seems to be warning her off the case. With help from her attorney husband, Travis, she sets out to examine the tangled Rankin family ties that may or may not provide the answer. In her quest for the killer, Antonia uses the skills she's acquired through FBI training and her experience as a forensic photographer.

She's also aided and abetted by her father, a university professor whose anger toward the agrichemical business has led him to blow up the college's greenhouse.

Travis, meanwhile, is defending a wife accused of having murdered her abusive husband. In the small town of Chastity Creek, this creates animosity toward the Buchanans from the victim's family. To add to the mix of mysteries, there's a homeless Vietnam vet with his own agenda, which may or may not relate to Matilda's death.

The more deeply Antonia delves into the Rankin family background, the more potential suspects are revealed, including Matilda's son, who is on the verge of bankruptcy; a sister estranged from the family; and even Matilda's daughter, who is Antonia's longtime friend. Not only must Antonia look at the current murder, she must dig deep into the past to uncover possible motives. The investigation turns deadly when she comes too close to discovering the killer.

In the fictional Chastity Creek located on the St. Johns River somewhere between Elkton and Palatka, author Nancy Quatrano has created a believable small-town atmosphere in which relationships overlap and old secrets are bound to come to light sooner or later. The plot's many intricacies will keep readers on edge until the very end. Quatrano plans "Murder in Black and White" as the first of the Point and Shoot Mystery Series.

Dear Readers,

Welcome to Chastity Creek, Florida, circa 2003, and thanks for reading *MURDER IN BLACK AND WHITE*. I hope you'll enjoy getting to know Antonia, affectionately known as AJ, and her husband Travis, as well as the rest of the people in "the Creek."

Chastity Creek is a fictitious northeast Florida town, fashioned after several of my favorite Old Florida towns, and strategically located close to the St. Johns River. Its people are the wonderful native Floridians I've come to know since relocating here: hard working, God-fearing people who care about their neighbors, and mostly mind their business, but will rush to your aid if needed.

When the manuscript won the Royal Palm Literary Fiction Award for the Unpublished Mystery category, I was over the moon about that!

If you enjoyed this story, please post a review on Amazon or any of the book review sites. We'd appreciate it. And if you have comments about how to make the series a better read for you, please email me: nancy@NLQuatrano.com and I'll be sure to get back to you.

Be well and again, thanks for taking a chance on this book. I appreciate your time and your feedback!

*N. L. Quatrano*

## DEDICATION and APPRECIATION

This book is dedicated to my critique group which read so many versions of this mystery that they've probably given up the genre as a result. Thanks Daria, Gail and Karen for never giving up on me or this book. I love you ladies!

And, to my beautiful daughters, Jackie Lewis, Jackie Lyn Barry and Eryka McCarthy, for cheering me on during the late nights and early mornings and many years of working on this novel. Your faith in me is only surpassed by mine in each of you. I love you, my daughters.

And, to the lovely and patient Anne Walradt who taught me more things about powerful writing, grammar, grace and determination than any other person in my life. Thank you so much.

And to the homeless in our nation, I'm sorry. But for God's grace, I have almost been there myself, more than once. May God grant you peace, joy, comfort and all of your needs.

# CHAPTER ONE

I shoot people for a living.

But I did not shoot the local matriarch, Matilda Renkin.

Matilda's a fixture. An icon. And, in some ways, my friend.

But last Friday, she went missing from our dysfunctional, Spanish Moss-laden community of Chastity Creek. In this tiny Northeast Florida town, that was bigger news than the local potato launching competition.

So, despite the fact that I had breakfast with her the day before her daughter reported her missing, I had nothing to do with her disappearance. I'm worried as hell about her, though. Disappearing is not Matilda's style.

My name is Antonia Jereaux Buchanan, and in addition to being a private investigator for several insurance companies and my husband's law practice, I'm a professional photographer. Since photography is what I really love, I shoot my Nikon more than my Smith and Wesson.

I was at loose ends Monday morning because I was supposed to meet Matilda for breakfast, but she's still missing. I called her in hopes she'd returned home since last Friday, but I didn't get an answer. Rocking in my Adirondack chair, I wondered what I could do to help. Law enforcement agencies tend to be a bit territorial about their investigations, so I'm careful about sticking my nose in things.

*Where can the woman be?*

The front gardens needed to be trimmed and mulched which would keep me from grinding my teeth, and at some point, I planned to paint the new gingerbread trim on the front porch in a Key West shade of purple. But with feeling so apprehensive I opted to sit and rock on the porch.

A car door slammed, and I looked up from my coffee cup. Betty Renkin Nichols strode up the sidewalk to the porch steps on my refurbished Victorian cottage. Slender shoulders stiff, dimpled chin in the air. She didn't look happy. *This isn't going to be fun...*

"Morning, Betty. What can I do for you?"

She stuck her flamingo-pink-painted index finger in my face. "My mother hires you for some oddball reason, and suddenly she's missing." Her nostrils flared. "What did she want?"

I gestured for her to sit in the rocker next to mine, but she shook her head. *Whatever.* "She wants me to do a photographic memoir of Chastity Creek."

Betty glared at me, and I tried for a non-confrontational expression. She needed a friend, not a fight. "She hired AJ the photographer, not the investigator?"

"That's right. She didn't hire me to investigate anything or anyone. Do you think someone should be investigated?"

Betty clutched her jacket around her as though the sixty-five-degree November morning was chilling her to the bone. She shook her blonde head vigorously, the perfect pageboy swaying like a Palomino's mane.

"No, of course not. I just thought since you were the last one who saw her and she asked you to come to the house, maybe…"

"Do you think your mother was in some kind of danger?" I sipped my now-cool coffee and looked out across the front lawn to the Indian Hawthorne hedge that no longer sported its small white flowers. I'd learned the power of silence while in the FBI, a long time ago.

She dropped into the rocker and sighed. "I'm sure that's silly. I was just wondering, that's all. It's not like her to just vanish."

"I agree with you, doesn't seem like the Matilda I know either. But I'm gonna tell you what I told the Sheriff's office yesterday. Matilda and I discussed a photographic documentary of Chastity Creek, the Renkin family history, and local landmarks, things like that. She sees Chastity Creek and the rest of old Florida changing and not necessarily for the good. She wants to preserve the history in photos."

"Did you start it yet?" Betty's rigid jaw seemed to relax a little. Her light blue eyes filled with tears that threatened to spill over.

I leaned forward and handed her the napkin from under my coffee cup. I knew how much she loved her mom. I also knew she wouldn't appreciate my sympathy, at least not right now.

"I took her retainer, gave her an outline of how I'd like to proceed, and we were supposed to meet this morning to review the outline. Go over some names. I didn't plan on doing much until she approved the plan."

"Do you remember any of the names she gave you? Does anyone know she wants you to do this? Maybe somebody is trying to protect some awful secret."

"I have the names inside. The church ladies, the book club ladies, some names I didn't recognize-think they are in the Jacksonville area now. I didn't talk to anyone yet. I don't know if your mother did or not."

"Can I see the outline?" she asked softly.

"Sure. Matilda's copy should have been at her house. Didn't you see it there?" I'd placed it in the middle of her desk in the library.

I didn't notice anything, but then I wasn't really looking for it, either. She was supposed to be home making lunch when I arrived Friday. Her car was there but she wasn't. No note, nothing." She sucked in a ragged breath. "I got delayed in Orange Park and arrived late. Maybe if I'd been on time, she would still be here."

"I'm sure that's not the case." I owed Matilda and I wanted Betty to know I would help if I could. "It's not like your mother, that's true. If she makes an appointment, she keeps it." I laughed. "Remember the time when she broke her foot and she showed up at the football game anyway? She didn't even tell us it hurt until we were in the car going home."

Tears slipped down her face. "I remember. She didn't want to disappoint us. She was often hurting and never said anything to anyone." Betty used the tattered napkin to dab at her face. "I didn't come here to hash over old times, AJ. Can I have your notes?"

"Sure, come on in. I'll print you a copy."

I held open the aqua-painted screen door, then led the way toward the long hallway to my office.

"Want a cup of coffee?" I asked, detouring through the kitchen to pour myself a fresh cup.

"No. Just the notes. I've *got* to find my mother."

I turned and looked at her. Her stress was tangible, but there was something else, too. "The Sheriff's doing everything he can. How about we go over that list together and you let me know if you pick up a clue somewhere?" I placed my mug on the counter. "Someone had to see her leave, especially if she didn't drive…"

She flapped her arms like a pelican getting ready to soar over the Intracoastal. "I don't *need* your help. Just give me the damned outline."

I shrugged and went into my office. Okay with me if she wanted to fly solo. It wasn't like we were best friends or anything. I pulled up the file, sent it to the printer and in two minutes I handed her a freshly-printed copy.

"Thanks." She turned on her heel and fled out of the room.

The wooden door slammed behind her when she swooped out of the house.

\*\*\*

Hours later the phone rang, jostling me out of my focused pursuit of perfection. Lifting my fingers from the keyboard, I hit the speaker button on my phone.

"Hey, Trouble. What are you doing?" The New Jersey twang of my cop-turned-lawyer husband always made me smile.

"Finishing up the O'Malley file for Farleigh Insurance. Where are you?"

"I'm on Interstate 10 heading east from Tallahassee. Should be home around six."

"How'd it go with the State's Attorney?"

"Not as badly as it could have. This is clearly a case of an abused woman defending herself. Thanks to the witnesses you found, the SA's not going for man one. I think we'll get her justice. After six months in jail, it's about time, right?"

"Spoken like a true defender of the underdog, Crimestopper." I chuckled, feeling good on his behalf. Justice was very important to my husband. Could say it was almost an obsession. "Glad to hear it's going to work out for her."

"Me, too. A few more wins and my faith in our judicial system may begin to mend."

We were both quiet. He had powerful reasons to doubt the system he had once believed in so passionately. We both did, we just didn't discuss them much.

"Nice to hear that, too. What would you like to eat tonight?" I asked.

"Don't bother with anything. We'll go to Corky Bells and have dinner on the river, how about that?"

"Great idea. Believe they may have music tonight, too." *Nothing like a cod dinner and country music.* "I'll see you when you get home."

I shut off the speaker, bound the report in a folder, printed the appropriate labels from my computer, and got it ready to mail.

I glanced at my copy of Matilda's project outline. Maybe if I believed strongly enough, she'd return safe and sound with a wonderful adventure story. I could drive to the old mill, snap some baseline photos before I lost the light, and be home in plenty of time to meet Travis for dinner.

*** 

I drove my restored jet-black Corvette across the cracked concrete apron that bridged the culvert in front of the desolate Renkin Paper Mill. Once a bustling factory that employed a hundred people, now it sat deserted and melancholy as the St. Johns River flowed by.

Deep green Kudzu vines, pale Queen Anne's lace plants, and faded ferns adorned the ground at the base of the battered red brick walls and broken windows. I stood and listened as the wind rustled through the dried fronds on the tall palms. Somewhere along the riverbank frogs called out from their perches in the sun, and cardinals chirped in the woods surrounding the mill. I could smell marshy, low-water decay mixed with pine and dried leaves. *Very spooky place*. I took a deep breath and tried the door.

The door wouldn't budge, even when I slammed my shoulder against it. *Damn that hurt*.

I placed my camera kit on the ground and stomped around loudly, hoping to discourage any slithering inhabitants. I am so scared of snakes that the last time I saw one I almost hyperventilated. Poisonous or not, I'm not hanging around to identify them. I combined some half-hearted Karate jumps with old-fashioned boot pounding and worked up the nerve to approach a broken window I could reach.

I pulled my revolver from an outer pocket on the camera bag and moved it into my jacket. I was more afraid of critters than humans, but if my FBI training had taught me anything at all, it was always better to be prepared for the unexpected.

I tossed my bag through the window frame. Then I pulled myself through the opening, shimmied across the rusty rail, and tumbled two feet to the floor. I got to my feet and brushed myself off, only to find a jagged tear in my jeans just above the left knee. No blood, but the pants were wrecked. *Great*.

The bank of windows along the west side provided a warm light only available when the sun is on the wane. I pulled my camera out and began to rapid shoot.

In the back corner of the first floor, I spotted cardboard, old clothing and a ragged green blanket–a typical homeless person's nest. *Someone was calling this home*. I picked my way across the room to determine if it was recent or old, my heart beating faster in my chest. I didn't need to scare the life out of a homeless person or lose mine to someone I didn't see coming.

The coffee cup had dregs in the bottom, but no mold or insects. *Hasn't been here long*. I sniffed the air, but I didn't detect any unwashed human body odor.

I scanned the area and felt I wasn't alone. My senses were on alert. I spotted the concrete stairs to the second floor and a faded stencil on the wall behind them that pointed to *OFFICES*.

I collected my bag and headed up the steps. Before I reached the landing, I heard a shuffling below me and froze. I held my breath, tucked my bag on the step, and eased back down the stairs as quietly as I could.

A stooped male figure was on all fours below the window I'd used to get inside. I slipped my hand inside my jacket pocket ready to reach for my gun, when he stood and looked at me. His matted brown hair and beard framed startled eyes.

For a long moment, he stared at me as though I was an apparition. The color drained from his face, his mouth opened and then he turned and dove through the window faster than my Nikon could shoot a photo.

"Hey," I called to his back. I ran to the window, just in time to see him crash into the mirror on my car. The impact spun him around, but he caught himself and sent a hurried look in my direction. Then his tattered shirt tails were flapping in the breeze behind him. Aside from maybe his height and a guess on hair color, I had no good description of the squatter.

I eased back from the window and crouched there for a few minutes, listening for returning footsteps. I'd probably scared him more than he scared me, but I'd keep my ears open and my gun handy, just the same. I picked up my bag and climbed the rusted steps to the second floor.

Seven wooden, once-white doors stood open, each framed in a rusted steel doorframe. A six-by-eight steel sign at the end of the hallway identified Richard Renkin's office. I closed my eyes to capture the lingering memories that always inhabit structures that once contained human beings.

*Men and women worked here in the heat, day after day to take home their twenty-five dollars a week. They had affairs. They lost children and parents and spouses, and one day they all lost their jobs.*

I focused my camera to grab as much as the shadowy light would permit and moved down the hallway.

I nudged open a door to my right marked "PAYROLL" and took some photos of the battered grey steel desks. Lined up like soldiers in the middle of the room, I could almost hear the adding machines clacking away and the typewriters used to put employee names on

11

their pay envelopes. I snapped a shot of the rusted Lucky Strike sign on the wall at the far end of the room.

I backed out of there and moved toward the boss's office. That door had a grime-coated glass pane in the middle of it where all the others were solid. I bumped it open with the toe of my boot and then my brain caught up with the shutter on my camera and the smell of decaying human being. I struggled to swallow past the lump in my throat.

Slumped over the huge mahogany desk, head turned toward the windows, her arms hung limp at her side. She was in the center of my long lens.

In stark contrast to the absence of life all around it, a determined coral vine bloomed through a broken window beside the desk.

Matilda Renkin was dead.

## CHAPTER TWO

Outside the mill, red and blue lights flashed in the darkness. My head throbbed and I shook with a chill that went into my bones.

"Mrs. Buchanan, all the paperwork for your gun is in order. Thanks for your patience while we sort all this out."

The deputy handed my revolver back to me and watched me slip it into my purse. We stood quietly side by side, facing the old building.

I stared at the deputy's business card, wishing someone else had discovered Matilda's body. For the second time in less than a week, I had to respond to questions about me and Matilda that were tough to answer. *What is my relationship to the deceased?*

I'd known when she and I talked last week that there was probably more to her request than she'd told me. I had no idea what her reservations were, though. Now I was sorry I hadn't pushed her for more information. *Maybe she'd be alive.*

A commotion behind us barely registered in my mind until I heard a familiar voice.

"Antonia! Are you okay?"

Strong hands gripped my shoulders and turned me around. My husband was looking as concerned as I'd seen in quite a while.

I felt tears building and swallowed. "I'm just rattled, that's all. And sad. I'm not sure what I expected to find today, but it wasn't Matilda." I took a deep breath and shook my head. "I was hoping she'd show up safe with a reasonable explanation for being gone."

Travis pulled me against his chest and wrapped his arms around me, resting his chin on the top of my head. No matter how bad things got, when I was with him, everything seemed better. The tears were closer, but I didn't care. Travis was the one person I could cry with.

"I know, honey. When you called me, I couldn't believe it myself."

"Mr. Buchanan, sir?" a tall deputy asked.

"Yes, I'm Travis. Can I take her home? I'll have a truck come for the car if that's all right."

"There's blood all over the side of the car, but FDLE says it isn't part of the crime scene, so they won't impound it. They've taken photos and swabbed it. Sheriff says she can go home and we'll talk to her later if we need to. We've got her statement."

"Blood?" Travis whispered, looking down at me.

I sighed. I felt like I had lead weights sitting on my chest. "I startled a homeless guy. He could have cut himself getting away from me, I guess. The blood on the car isn't mine or Matilda's, so stop worrying, okay?"

I pulled away from him and turned around to face the old brick building, just in time to watch the county coroner's people wheel the gurney carrying Matilda's bagged corpse down the cracked and overgrown walkway to the wagon. They wouldn't be using sirens and lights for this ride. I thought about Betty and shivered again.

Travis stepped away from me and made a phone call which I assumed was to Mikey's Towing. I stared at the building again. It held clues to what had happened.

"Sir, sir! You can't go…," shouted a deputy.

I whirled around and then jumped backward about four feet in the face of pure fury, only to slam into my husband.

"You bitch. You lying, conniving bitch. I'm going to kill you!"

I felt Travis move beside me. The deputy pulled me to the side so he and Travis were between me and the red-faced mountain charging my way. I peeked around Travis's shoulder.

"Bobby Joe?" I said, in disbelief. "Doesn't your family have enough trouble, already?"

Since I could smell the whiskey on his breath from ten feet away, I was thankful for the two men playing sentinels. I'm five nine, pushing a hundred sixty pounds, and I can take pretty good care of myself, but Bobby Joe was as massive as an offensive lineman. He could definitely hurt me.

"Sir, this is a crime scene. You need to go back beyond that yellow tape. If you don't leave on your own, you'll be arrested."

"Davis Shane, you was in short pants when I were beatin' your daddy at pool. Don't use that 'sir' crap on me. You ain't going to arrest me for nothin'."

"I'm sorry Bobby Joe, but I sure will. You've been drinking, you just threatened a witness, and you don't belong here. I hope you weren't driving…"

"You don't worry about my driving. You gonna arrest this bitch and her Yankee husband?"

"No sir, I'm going to arrest you." With that, Deputy Shane deftly grabbed Bobby's left arm, twisted him around with it, and had handcuffs on him before he could close his big mouth.

Travis stepped back to stand beside me and looked mad enough to strangle the man. "What's that all about?" he asked out the side of his mouth.

I wrinkled my nose. "Bobby Joe Fletcher is Brian Donovan's first cousin. He believes your client murdered his best friend in cold blood."

"Why didn't you tell me that a little earlier?"

16

"I was going to fill you in on several things over dinner tonight. I only made the connection around noon today."

"Great. Since he knows the deputy, I'm going to assume he's a local fellow. Are there more of them?"

I nodded and stuffed my hands deep into my jacket pockets. "He's the only one that thinks that Margie's a murderer, though. He and Donovan were raised by the same grandmother, over in Palatka. Lived here most of their lives. He's in Gainesville now where all the rest of the family lives. I can't explain how he found me out here, though."

Deputy Shane watched as three younger officers wrestled Bobby Joe into the back seat of a white car identified by dark green lettering: SHERIFF.

He looked at me. "How many *other* people you think might be riled up at you, Mrs. Buchanan?"

Travis shrugged, answering before I could. That was the lawyer in him, I guess. I can get myself into hot water faster than a gator can snag a fish and he knows it.

"No telling, really. There's unfinished business from her Washington days, several local wife-beaters who did time thanks to her investigations, and I'm sure there could be some hometown folks upset that she went and married a Yankee. Twice, actually. However, this," he waved his hand toward the car with the cage in the back, "has more to do with a case I'm defending than with my bride, I'm glad to say."

The deputy shook his head, his eyes narrowing as he looked closely at me. "Now I know why you look so familiar. You're the investigator that helped out a few of the women at the shelter, right?"

"That's me." I hoped he would let it drop.

"And you're defending Margie Donovan, right?" he asked Travis.

"Right."

He shook Travis's hand and then mine. "If you can come to the office tomorrow, we'll get the artist to work with you on the transient," he said, looking at me. "Whatever help you can give us is appreciated."

He turned on his highly polished black boots and I spotted the tow truck operator waiting to get down the battered drive to retrieve my car. Travis wrapped an arm around my shoulder.

"Let's go get something to eat. Then it's home to bed. Tomorrow you'll have to face Betty."

## CHAPTER THREE

My Cajun grandmother claimed to have "the sight," but I think my New Jersey-bred husband has it, too. Travis was right as rain about Betty. When I got to the Putnam County Sheriff's office to work on the sketch of the bearded man, Betty was waiting for me.

"You told me you didn't know where she was," she snarled, charging out of the chair. The coroner's assistant moved to stop her, but I waved him off.

"I'm sorry about your mother, Betty. And I wasn't lying to you when we talked. I had no idea she even went to the mill anymore. My finding her was completely accidental."

Her usually flawless makeup was streaked by tear tracks, her crystal-blue eyes red-rimmed and bloodshot. Grief rolled off her like fog off the river. She all but collapsed into the wooden chair, and the assistant handed her a box of tissues.

19

"I just can't believe this. She can't be dead. She just can't be dead. It's too soon…," she sobbed, rocking back and forth in the chair.

I crouched down in front of her but didn't touch her. A daughter's grief was something I was personally familiar with. My heart ached for her and I slowly exhaled.

"I know, Betty. I can't believe it either, but they may find out that she died of natural causes, you know. Maybe she had some condition you didn't know about."

She wiped at her face. Anger and grief formed a mixed mask of emotion. "I'm not just her daughter, I'm an RN. No medicine bottles around her house. Nothing observable-no shortness of breath, no bad coloring—it just doesn't make sense."

I straightened. "Remember my mother? She took the cookies out of the oven and dropped dead. Mom and the cookies were still warm when I got home from school. You don't get warnings with things like aneurysms, strokes, stuff like that. It's awful and I know how shocking it can be, but any of those is a possibility."

She clenched her fists in her lap, soggy tissues gripped tight in her fingers. "I know. I just can't believe that I didn't spend enough time with her to notice."

"Where's Michael?" I wondered why her husband wasn't around to help her through the identification process.

"He's on his way back from Arizona right now. I talked to him at six this morning and the flights are delayed with an early snowstorm in Iowa or Indiana or some damned mid-west state."

"Did you call Richard, yet? I'm sure he'd want to get out here."

"I called him twice. Got my sister-in-law the second time, but she said he was travelling. She promised to tell him what happened when he called home." She looked at her hands. "I'm not sure he'd come, anyway."

"I know there never seemed to be any love lost between them, but I'm sure he'd want to help you with this."

Her laugh was bitter, almost a snort. "He hated my guts. Hated me more than he hated our mother. To be honest with you, I doubt he'll come out here, even for her funeral."

A tall administrative person in a starched white Sheriff's Office shirt came in to let me know the artist was ready. I picked up my jacket and purse.

"If you need me for anything Betty, just let me know, okay?"

She nodded and stood. Her proud shoulders drooped and she moved like a woman in her eighties. I understood all too well the weight of that kind of grief. I still bore some of my own, even though my mother had died more than twenty years ago.

\*\*\*

21

Travis joined me in the squad room where I worked with the artist for several hours.

When all was said and done, the sketch was of a thousand faceless men who wandered the country and lived wherever they could. Recent VA surveys have established that many of these men in our area are veterans with a wide range of medical conditions that go untreated. Travis gave free legal help to every one of them that walked into his office, so I was well versed in the statistics. But was the man at the mill one of those? I didn't have any idea.

Witness or a killer? A completely innocent man who'd found a relatively safe place to sleep for a few days? I hadn't been able to look him in the eye for longer than a split second, not long enough to determine his eye color let alone his life story.

I knew well how life could change in a split second though. I'd lost my mother, and a husband, in just about that amount of time. Not long slow agonizing deaths at least, but life-crushing for the survivors.

I decided long ago that life should come with one warning: "Buckle Up."

# CHAPTER FOUR

Wednesday began as one of those brilliant November mornings that make you utter a prayer of thanks to God for giving you another day, even if you claim you don't believe in God. The air was crisp and clean, the sun just warm enough to let you get by with a lightweight jacket.

*Gonna get ugly, though.* Matilda's body would be autopsied today.

I sat in my office and created a file to keep the notes from my last conversation with Matilda. Her resigned suspicions that her children were more concerned with her assets than her happiness; the ghost of her secret love; her sorrow over the fact that when she died, no one would know or care about the history of Chastity Creek or old Florida.

As a photojournalist, I could empathize with her concerns about lost eras. It was the main reason I agreed to the project.

I worked for an hour before Travis called to check in, then wandered into the kitchen, and poured another coffee. I watched the crimson cardinals flitting around the bird feeder in the garden, their red almost blending with the early blooming poinsettias that rimmed the back yard.

But there was work to be done in the real world, like acquiring information on Nathan and maybe Matilda's dead husband. I went back to the office, fired up my computer, bypassed CNN and Weather.com, and went right into my genealogy and public record data bases.

Mesters. Date of birth, no death certificate on record which in and of itself didn't mean much. I didn't have a social security number or middle initial which meant I couldn't use a Social Security trace. Travis had mentioned that old man Renkin had fired Nathan from the factory, so I assumed he'd eventually left the area and gone on to live happily ever after somewhere else. The most puzzling aspect was Matilda's reference to Nathan's ghost which of course would mean he was no longer among the living. And maybe he hadn't left the area. Or maybe she was just that sure he wouldn't have left her behind, even in death.

No information listed before or after the date of his dismissal. Hell, I still wasn't clear why Matilda had almost hinted that he haunted the factory in a ghostly state. Had he been happy there? Had they made love there? Had he been killed there? Matilda had evaded my questions entirely. *This is going to make me crazy.*

I printed what I'd unearthed and moved to the DMV and criminal sites. For a fee of course, a private investigator can obtain a lot of data on a person and never leave the comforts of home.

I completed all of the information I had available, authorized the charges to my account and moved on to my criminal sites. Again, I entered Nathan's name, date of birth and last known residence. Nada. Nothing. Okay, so all that meant was that he didn't have a criminal record. Odd to put in a name on the Internet and get virtually no information. But, prior to 1980, we didn't have computers available in every business or household. The State Department and NASA had them of course, but they took up a room the size of the Tallahassee State Assembly.

I put Mesters aside and ran the same inquiries on Richard Renkin, Sr. At least a hundred references on him. Businessman of the Year in 1985, '87 and '88. Big with the town council. In a small town, he was a big man. Never the mayor, mind you, but on paper, he looked like Mr. Class A Joe Citizen which of course I knew wasn't exactly true. I saved the data to a file, switched back to my browser and sat back to enjoy my coffee. I had some good stuff, even though I didn't have all I needed.

My relaxed but focused session was interrupted by someone knocking on the kitchen door. I picked up my mug and padded barefoot through the house.

Betty stood on the back porch, looking away from the house. I pulled the door open. "How you doing, girl?"

Her smile was fragile, and she'd aged since I'd talked with her Monday. I motioned for her to come in.

We sat on the old church pew Travis and I had turned into our breakfast nook. Betty sat with her hands folded in front of her.

"Coffee? Or I've got tea and hot chocolate."

She looked as though she didn't hear me, but finally she nodded. "Hot chocolate would be great. Got any marshmallows?"

I laughed. "What good would hot chocolate be without them?"

I put on a saucepan of milk and pulled out the largest mug in the cabinet. Rummaging around the kitchen, I found Travis's stash of Girl Scout cookies and tossed a package of Trefoils and a box of Thin Mints on the table.

"Remember that sleep over at Michelina's house? What was that – our junior year?" she asked.

"Yeah, we almost burned the house down roasting marshmallows over candles in her bedroom."

Betty laughed. "You and Donna tossed your lemonades at the flames which knocked the candle over and set the cat on fire."

"When we tried to catch the cat, the dog tripped Michelina, and she sprained her ankle." I dumped the cocoa into the pan and whisked it with the milk and then poured it into the cup, adding the marshmallows on top.

Betty inhaled the steaming fragrance while I sat down and grabbed a couple of Thin Mints.

"Who the hell caught the cat? I can't remember," I asked.

Betty shook her head. "I don't remember, either. Might have been Donna, though. She was always the fast one."

For a few minutes, we sat together, sharing a childhood snack and some faded memories. The laughter felt good.

"I was a pretty big pain in the ass in high school, wasn't I?" she asked quietly, looking me in the eye.

"You were certainly a pain in *my* ass more than once. But then again, I suppose it wasn't your fault that every boy in the school drooled when you walked by."

I'd probably lost at least six boyfriends to the curvaceous and lively Betty Renkin between junior high school and high school graduation.

"Actually, there were times when I really just wanted to be like everyone else, you know. But I had big boobs, was a Renkin, and probably considered pretty well off."

"Well, your mom tried to keep us all grounded. She wanted us to be proud of ourselves, our town, and our Florida heritage. Never took any crap from the rednecks or the good old boys, either."

She put down her cocoa. "My mother was very strict about respect and responsibility, not so big on the mushy-type stuff, but she loved us like crazy."

I shook my head. "She loved everyone in this town like they were family. When my mother died and Papa had his meltdown, she made sure the county put me into foster care right here in town with the Lukers. She didn't have to do that, but she considered it her duty to us."

"Was that really a good thing, though? Their kid Martin was only twelve, but he was mean as a rattlesnake with a hangover. Broke your arm, didn't he?"

"Sure did—I was trying to keep him from killing their dog. He was a sick kid. Probably ended up a serial killer somewhere."

"Nope. He was shot by the cops over in Ocala about ten years ago. You were gone by then, but I think he tried to run down a cop, and they shot him. I remember thinking I didn't even have to be there to know he really deserved it."

"Betty," I started, "your mom was upset about something with you and Richie. I didn't want to pry when she and I were talking, but what was that about?"

She stirred the cooled cocoa and watched the swirls around the spoon. "Richie's been talking about moving her to Arizona to be by him. He found a really nice, assisted living place and wanted her to sell everything and move there."

"Why?" I asked.

She shrugged. "Seriously? He's in some kind of big trouble and I think he needs Mother's money. And as much as she loved Chastity Creek and all it stands for, she was really tempted to leave, I think. She's always wanted him to love her, even a little."

"What kind of trouble's he in?"

"I don't understand it all. Something to do with a securities company he worked for. I didn't ask Mother, but I heard her talking with her attorneys when I visited a couple of months ago. It sounded pretty serious."

She glanced at her watch and snagged one more cookie from the box. "I gotta go. Michael and I are going to dinner in St. Augustine." She stood and slipped into her jacket. "I'm really sorry I snapped at you the other day. I'm about out of my mind with all this."

She glanced at her hands and then at me. "Will you do the photo project anyway? For me? If it was important for my mother, it's important to me, too. I'd like you to do it. Track down our illustrious history and document it for all time. Will you?"

I thought about twenty seconds. "I will. And thanks. It should be fascinating and what a nice tribute to your family."

She looked relieved. "Tomorrow I'm going to start funeral arrangements for Mother."

"Did anyone call you with the autopsy results yet?" I asked as I cleared the table.

"Yeah. Coroner says Mother died of heart failure. Said she probably died pretty much right away."

"I'm glad you have an answer, anyway. And I'm glad it's nothing sinister." I didn't mention that we still had the problem of how she got there....

She picked up her purse and straightened her denim jacket, her blue eyes flashing.

"You know what I think, AJ? I think they're dead wrong."

So did I.

## CHAPTER FIVE

"You have got to be kidding me," Travis moaned. He tossed the Palatka Daily News on the kitchen counter.

"What's the matter?" I asked over my shoulder as I flipped the French toast on the griddle.

"When did you talk to your father last?"

"Two days ago, I think. Why?" I reached into the refrigerator, pulled out the orange juice, and filled two glasses.

"Well, the two of you are front page news, this morning. You for finding Matilda…"

The phone rang, interrupting him. Puzzled, I hit the speaker button on the phone and answered without even looking at the caller ID.

"This is the Gainesville Fire Department. Looking for Antonia Jereaux."

"This is her. Can I help you with something?"

His silence spoke volumes. My father. My heart just about dropped into my stomach as I turned off the griddle and tossed the spatula in the sink.

Travis placed the newspaper in front of me, but I was not focused on it. "What is it? Is my father all right?"

"He's fine, Ms. Jereaux. There's been an accident, though."

"What kind of accident?"

Travis tapped me on the arm.

"I'm going to let him tell you about it. Here he is, ma'am."

When he didn't speak to me, I snapped at him. "Papa, what in the world is going on?"

"Well, I was working on a new type of organic fertilizer and there was a little problem. Actually, sort of an explosion."

Jabbing his finger at the bottom half of the newspaper in an attempt to get my attention, Travis directed me to my father's shocked face under an equally shocking headline: "Exploding Greenhouse."

"Papa, you weren't hurt, were you? Do you need to go to the hospital?"

"Antonia, I blew up my garden, but I did not sustain any injury. I don't need the hospital. I would like you to come get me, however. I cannot stay in the house the way it is and Harry only has the one bedroom."

I groaned and shook my head. "I just saw the paper and I understand." It was eight-thirty a.m. and Gainesville was an hour away. "We'll be there before eleven, Papa. Can you go to Harry's and we'll pick you up there?" His neighbor across the street was a Mr. Roger's lookalike and he adored my father.

"These nice firemen will call him for me. I'll pack some clothes and be waiting." The call disconnected and the dial tone filled our kitchen.

I stared at our uneaten breakfast and sighed. *At least he's okay...* I nodded at my husband and dashed upstairs to shower and dress.

When I got out of the shower, Travis was waiting for me with a fluffy towel and my coffee. I scrubbed my short hair for a moment and wrapped the towel around me before dropping onto the paisley-covered chaise in the corner.

"What in the world are we going to do about this?"

Travis leaned in the doorway, legs crossed at the ankles, arms folded on his chest. His gray eyes twinkled, and I couldn't help but laugh. He always found a way to make me feel better.

"We'll figure it out when we see how bad it is."

"How could he do this? How in the world could he risk his position at the university? He's going to be known as a mad scientist if he's not careful."

"Things are rarely what they seem on the surface, remember that. And do you really think your dad cares what people think? About as much as you do." He winked.

"You sound just like him, you know." I finished my coffee and got to my feet.

"That's why you love me, Sweety," he said, dropping his clothes on the floor and climbing into the antique claw-footed tub for a shower of his own.

I was sorely tempted to climb back in that tub.

\*\*\*

Since my car was in the shop getting the mirror replaced, we locked up the house and climbed into his Ford F250. My Yankee truly loved his big pickup truck.

"So, when will you know about Margie Donovan?" I asked when we'd driven in silence almost thirty minutes. The day was warm, gray, and sunless; the trees muted with their fall color changes.

"We'll meet with the judge in chambers next Tuesday. I've made a motion to request we waive a jury trial, and he and the State's Attorney are finally agreeable. Donovan's family is okay with it, so I don't see why it won't be accepted."

"How's she holding up? Anything she needs that I can take to her when I visit next time?"

He shook his head. "After almost six months behind bars, she probably needs everything, but they don't allow much more than books, really. You can take her some new clothes and makeup before we go see the judge if she wants you to."

"I'll get over there tomorrow and check in with her. How bad is the worst-case scenario?"

"Depends on the judge. The state's attorney is still looking over everything I left him, but he wasn't totally unreceptive to the involuntary manslaughter plea, given all the forensic evidence and the witnesses we deposed. Those depositions made a big difference. Of course, he could still go for voluntary manslaughter if he wants to. I don't think he will, though."

"Can you get her out of there before the court date?"

"Don't want to do that. She's safe, has a single cell where she can read and rest and she's not going to have peace anywhere else. No matter where she goes, she's going to be hounded by the press. And I'm nervous about Bobby Joe...he's a loose cannon if I ever met one. The kids are already in Alabama with Margie's mother. We did get the guardianship papers finished yesterday so she could legally care for them until Margie gets out."

"Well, I'm sure she's just glad that they're safe and away from all this. You did interviews with them. Do they talk about their father at all?"

"Not much." Travis reached for his travel mug and sipped his coffee. "Every time I mentioned him, they turned white and started to shake. We videotaped the interviews for the state and the judge, so we didn't have to put them through everything again. They're so traumatized, it's really very sad. Makes me mad as hell."

The green and white Florida landmark sign pointing the way to Marjorie Rawlings' State Park came and went in a blur as we drove along State Road 20.

I thought about Betty. And Matilda.

A lot of sad things going on these days.

The satellite radio played traditional bluegrass as we continued along, each with our own thoughts. Allison Krause was picking "Rocky Top" with Vince Gill when a phone call interrupted.

Travis hit the button on the steering wheel and nodded in my direction.

"AJ, are you there?"

"Betty? Yes, I'm here. Are you all right?"

"I'm doing okay, but I'm going to the mill. I want to hire you to go with me."

"I can't do that today. I've got some family business to handle." I shook my head. "Did you say hire me?"

"Yes, I did. I want you to investigate Mother's death. And, I read about your father. Your father was always so cool. I'm glad he wasn't hurt. Are you going to bring him here?"

"We are. I won't be back until after three probably."

"That's fine. I'll meet you at your place. But you and I are going to find out what really happened to my mother."

## CHAPTER SIX

"Papa, what in the world were you thinking?" I asked from the back seat of the truck which I shared with two large suitcases and what I guessed was a laptop.

He twisted around to look in my direction, his expression defiant. "Why aren't we researching more botanical solutions to everyday needs? I'll tell you why. The chemical companies are worried their cash cow will dry up. We're being poisoned by them, and Washington, D.C. is fully in favor of it."

Travis remained quiet, listening, and probably plotting a defense strategy if I knew my husband. I patted my father's arm and sat back in my seat. "That is very noble, but you could be in a lot of trouble."

"Maybe not so much, Antonia. It was an accident. This is why we pay insurance, yes?"

I could tell Travis was fighting a smile and that made me want to laugh myself. My father was a tenured botany professor at the University of Florida and at seventy-six years old, his once-dark hair was a thick, lustrous silver mantle. I'd inherited his black hair, hazel-colored eyes, and rather aristocratic nose. I hoped I'd own that beautiful silver color too, when it became my turn. Arguing of course, that I survived that long.

"Yes, Henri, that's why we buy insurance," said Travis.

I put my head back and closed my eyes. *Has everyone lost their minds?*

\*\*\*

Just outside the Putnam County line, the dashboard monitor in the truck lit up with another call. This one was from the Sheriff's Office.

"Mr. Buchanan?" a man inquired. "This is Shane Davis."

"Hello, deputy. What can we do for you this afternoon?" Travis reached over to turn up the speaker volume.

"Is your wife with you, sir? I haven't been able to reach her by phone today."

"Oh yes, she's here. She can hear you."

"Mrs. Buchanan, can you come in today to work with the artist," he asked. "We'd really like to get out a BOLO, see if we can find him."

I glanced at the dashboard display. It was two-thirty and Betty would be waiting for me in an hour. A logistical impossibility.

"We're about fifteen minutes outside town. We can be there in a few minutes. Will that work for you?"

"That'll be fine," he answered. "I get off at four, so this way I can take care of it myself. See you when you get here."

"Deputy Davis?" I asked before he could hang up.

"Yes, ma'am?"

"Please call me AJ. What is the status of Bobby Joe Fletcher?"

"He made bail this morning and headed back to Gainesville. You should probably apply for a restraining order just to be safe, though."

"A restraining order won't keep me safe, and we both know that. However, my gun will. Thanks for the information."

Travis hit the phone button and then turned the radio off.

"What is he talking about, Antonia?" my father asked. "Restrain whom?"

"A man who isn't very happy with me right now, that's all. Don't worry, Papa. This guy is a bully and he's

39

grieving the death of his cousin. He'll calm down, I'm sure. In the meantime, I'll keep a sharp eye out for him."

"Good. I come to your house, now and I'm going to build you a computer security system. It will help keep you safe."

"Papa, that's not necessary. Travis and I can take care of ourselves."

Travis cleared his throat. "Actually honey, I was thinking about an alarm system anyway. Your dad has the ASTA patented, right? Why not use our place for the prototype?"

I shook my head, not sure when they'd cooked up this approach, but I knew I was outranked and outnumbered. My father had become a techno-wizard around the time everyone was in a panic over Y2K. Why worry when you can invent a solution?

"How long will it take to wire the house and all that?" I hoped he'd say months and I could tell him to forget it.

"Maybe a week. I can give it all my attention. By the time I go back to school in January, your house will be able to keep you safe and my house will be back to normal, too."

"What if the university terminates you for the incident, Papa?"

"So what? Finding alternatives is the right thing to do. I'm too old for teaching these kids, anyway. They don't want to learn anything—they know everything already. This was going to be my last year, you know."

"I didn't realize that," I murmured. I was shocked that I was clueless. *Had he told me, and I hadn't heard him?* For the first time in my life, I saw my father as an old man. *How many years together did we have left?*

Travis pulled into the parking lot at the Sheriff's office, and we all piled out. I grabbed my shoulder bag from the back seat.

"You two don't need to come in unless you want to. I'll call Betty and have her pick me up on her way to the mill. I'll be home as soon as I can."

My father nodded, though he looked far from happy.

Travis leaned down to kiss me, then climbed back into the truck. I watched them until they were through the traffic light and moving south on SR17. Then my cell phone rang.

***

Forty minutes later, I was sitting next to Betty, and we were driving to the old mill.

She glanced at me. "I saw your car the other day. Almost looks like Mike Stratton's. Is there a history?"

"That 1968 Mako Shark Corvette is almost all that's left from my FBI life in Virginia. I was married to my late husband Rick.

"We spent many a weekend working on that car, restoring it with tender loving care and great attention to all the details. About the only other thing we did for recreation was go fishing at our cabin in the Blue Ridge Mountains. We were both law enforcement workaholics."

She chuckled and stopped at the traffic light. "I can understand that. Seems to run in my family. Not sure it's a good trait, though."

"I hear you. The older I get, the more I think about balance and time for enjoying life." I pulled out my phone and called Travis.

"Everything all right with my dad?" I asked. When he assured me all was as it should be, I listened to the usual admonitions about being careful, and staying in touch and promised that we'd be home before the sun set.

I looked over at Betty. "You know, it's bothering me that Matilda didn't take her car. Did she walk the eight miles to the mill?"

She wrinkled her nose. "No, she didn't walk, that I'd bet my paycheck on. See what I mean? This just doesn't add up."

Thinking about the ragged man who had surprised me the day I was there, I double checked to make sure my revolver was where I put it when I left the Sheriff's office.

\*\*\*

I put my pistol in my right jacket pocket and pulled two pair of latex gloves out of my purse and handed Betty a pair.

She watched me, her hair pulled back in a burgundy pony-tail and threaded through a Seminole baseball cap. She had on black hikers, faded denim jeans and a sequin-studded jean jacket. I pointed at her purse.

"Let's lock these up."

After slamming the trunk lid, she pocketed the car keys. "Do you think we'll need that?" she asked, motioning toward the pistol in my pocket.

"Probably not, but I'd rather have it and not need it than need it and not have it." I started toward the broken window that I'd used a few days earlier to gain access to the mill.

I went in first, scanning the area and listening for any movement. We seemed to be alone, so I motioned for Betty to join me. She got her jacket caught on the rusty window frame and cursed when it ripped free.

"I wrecked my jeans the other day—I forgot about that. Sorry."

Scowling in my direction, she brushed off her thighs and straightened up. Looking around, her expression changed from annoyed to wary. I stayed silent.

"Did you come here a lot when you were a kid?" I finally asked, as we pulled on the gloves.

"Not too often, but once in a while. When my father was out of town, we'd come here. Some very nice people worked here.

"Mrs. Carmichael would always give me homemade cookies from her lunch and there was a man named Nate, who was the foreman at one time. He was always wonderful to me and my mother. Mrs. Nelson always smelled like Chanel No. 5." She smiled at the memories.

I checked the side of the room where the homeless stuff had been a few days ago, but it had not been replaced.

"What happened to Nate?" I asked since I hadn't been able to find him on the internet yet.

"He died. Right after I graduated nursing school. He was such a good friend to me and mother. I think she was in love with him, actually." She moved toward the stairway and looked up. Without looking back at me, she asked the question I knew she'd ask. "You found Mom in his office, right?"

I nodded and walked toward her. I followed her up the stairs, keeping my ears open for the skittering of little mice feet or the shuffle of human ones. I stopped her when we reached the second floor.

"Let me go first. I'm not sure what the cops left behind."

I pushed open the grungy office door, holding my breath as I did so. No idea what I expected, but aside from fingerprint dust smudges, the room was much as I remembered it from the other day, except Matilda's body and the smell, was gone.

"Where was she?" Betty asked, looking around the office as though she'd see the ghost of her mother any minute.

"At the desk."

Betty walked over and reached out her hand, running her fingers gently over the old brass pull on the middle drawer. Reverently, she opened and closed each of the heavy maple drawers. I searched the floor starting from the door and working my way around the bank of windows back to the door. Not even a gum wrapper.

Betty knelt down in the opening where the desk chair had been. She pulled her keys from her pocket and lit up a tiny LED penlight.

She sucked in her breath and whispered my name. "Come here."

"What is it?" I asked, suddenly feeling as though we weren't alone. The hair on my neck raised and a shudder ran down my back.

She held up a thin, clear plastic cap of some sort. Looking closer I realized what it was but as a nurse, she already knew exactly what she held.

The cap of a hypodermic syringe.

"Let's get out of here," she said.

## CHAPTER SEVEN

Outside in the fading light, she popped the trunk of the car, and I wrapped the cap inside my glove, then tucked it in my purse.

"This is a good find, Betty. No telling if it's connected, but I'm surprised it was there. Unless someone dropped it there since the other night."

"You think people may be using the building to do drugs?"

"Who knows? Drug use goes on everywhere," I muttered. "If this was here the other night, the FDLE team should have found it. Since the place isn't totally boarded up, a squatter might have dropped it, though."

"Well, you said it was almost dark when they got here, maybe they didn't see it with their flashlights."

"You saw it with yours," I pointed out. "But then, we had light in the room today, so maybe you're right."

"So, *now* can I hire you to investigate this for me?" she asked, wriggling her slender body up onto the trunk of her Mustang.

"First of all, we don't know if there's anything to investigate. Secondly, I'm not going to charge you if there is something. Matilda was my client. I can't see any connection between the family documentary and her death, but I've seen weaker cases, so I'll keep an open mind."

"There might be more skeletons than you think," she muttered. "You can't work for free, AJ. Mike and I can afford to pay you."

She'd matured from a headstrong girl into a stubborn woman. But then, I could relate.

"Tell you what," I started, knowing arguing wouldn't solve anything. "If I incur expenses while investigating, you can reimburse me, okay? But I'm not charging you by the day. Your mother looked out for me when no one else could, so I owe her."

She thought a minute, then jumped off the car. "Okay. It's a deal." She stuck out her hand and we shook on it.

"Want to come home with me for dinner?"

She shook her head. "Gotta get home. Mike's expecting me."

"Have you talked to him about your suspicions? What's he think about all this?"

Swiping her hand across her forehead to push back a wayward strand of hair, she sighed. "He's so distracted lately I didn't bother him with it. He really liked my mother. He's as upset about her death as I am, but he'd never suspect that the coroner's report could be wrong." She pointed her finger at me. "Don't you go telling him, either."

I held up my hand. "I promise not to say a word." I wondered if Betty had to keep her grief hidden, too. "I'm going to run this cap to the Sheriff's department first thing in the morning."

She got into the car and slid the windows down. "Will you say something about my mother at her service? She was important to you, too."

"Well, we'll be there. If you really need me to do that, I will, but let's play it by ear, okay? Have you heard back from your brother yet?"

"No, and I'm not calling him again. If he doesn't want to deal with this, I don't care."

I nodded. "If you need anything, just call us, okay?"

She started the car. I looked one last time at the faded brick building in front of me.

Tired-red bottlebrushes displayed the last of their blooms on either side of the crumbling stairway to the front door, a testimony to the warmer fall weather. Again, I was struck by the power of life over death. The flora would not be deterred or diminished by the death of the mill or its owners.

I wondered if Betty would be as resilient.

***

The house was lit up when I arrived home. Betty dropped me at the curb and with a wave, she was gone.

"Hello," I called as I walked through the kitchen door. I could smell dinner, but I found the men in my office. The two of them were so engaged in whatever was on my computer they didn't hear me until I cleared my throat.

"What's up? You two look like you've lost your best friend." When neither one smiled, I got that sinking feeling in my gut. "Please don't tell me you've blown up my computer—"

Papa interrupted. "I was setting up some of the remote access files so I can program the automated security task assistant, but an email popped up on the screen. I thought I had clicked past it, but I must have activated the file. Quite an ugly message, I'm afraid."

His fingers flew across my keyboard to pull up my email account. The bright orange flames alongside the message were pretty eye catching. Add in that the originator address was PAINTBALL from an unknown source, and my curiosity gene was screaming. I wondered why my expensive spam filters hadn't caught the unknown address.

*Renkin and Renkin, dead as can be, that's all there is to this old story. Stop digging around or you will be next, good people need peace, leave them to rest.*

*Cute. A psychopathic poet.* At least no one could ever accuse me of having a humdrum life.

"Antonia, I do not like this. You have too many people angry with you. Something bad will happen."

I hugged my dad tightly. I knew how hard it was for him not to worry himself silly over me, so I tried to lighten it up.

"I'll be careful, and everything will be fine. Remember, we've had a lot of press the past few weeks, so just because it mentions the Renkin family, doesn't mean it has anything to do with them. But I promise not to take any unnecessary chances."

"I don't like it, *ma fille*." He saved the email and closed down the computer. "I'll have the security system up and running by the end of the weekend. Until then, you should not be running around by yourself."

Travis gave me a squeeze. "For the record, I don't like it either. But I promised not to smother you and I'm doing my best to keep that promise. So, dinner's ready, Trouble. How about setting the table? I'll open the wine."

Papa followed us into the kitchen and sat at the table. I noticed the eight-inch flat panel monitor now installed under my dish cabinet. "That's cool – what will it do?"

He smiled and pointed above the door. "ASTA will be wired to inside and outside cameras. From various places in the house, you'll be able to see any of those cameras. That," he pointed to the cabinet, "is one of the visual stations."

Getting up from the table, he moved to the kitchen door. "The doors and windows are wired, too. They will be motion activated and unless logged fingerprints scan at the door to gain entry, any disturbance at the doors or windows will trigger an alarm."

"A siren goes off or something?" I laughed, tucked the opened bottle of merlot under my arm, and collected wine glasses from the rack. "The neighbors will just love that."

"There will be an audible alarm, yes, but also the Sheriff will be notified immediately."

I lit the candles and poured the wine before sitting down between my husband and my dad. "Sort of like those Safe Touch guys, right?"

"Like this steak, ASTA is the ultimate...far superior to the average security system. She can answer your phone calls and your emails, she will protect your home, she can even light your fireplace, regulate the indoor temperature, and start the laundry if you'd like. Any electronic device can be added into the panel, so you have control from here or your phone."

"Wow, like having a live-in maid, secretary, and security guard huh? Very cool."

"That is why I used the word 'assistant' in the patent-Automated Security and Technology Assistant – it does more than just provide security."

"Well, 'smart' houses are featured on all the home shows, but they still come with a pretty big price tag. It'll be fun living with our very own version."

"ASTA is an affordable solution for people who own older homes, like you do. Thanks to wireless technology, the entire house doesn't have to be torn apart. I don't have the uninterrupted power module ready for this house, though. Maybe in a few weeks."

We finished dinner, chatting about Papa's adventurous invention and his ideas to market the system to security companies around the world. He might be retiring from academia, but he had no intention of sitting around idle.

Once we cleaned the kitchen, we settled into the parlor and Travis lit the gas fireplace. "Did you and Betty find anything at the mill today?" he asked, drawing me back to rest against his chest in the circle of his arms.

"Yes, a protective cap of a needle. Betty's been an RN for years. She said it looked like the type of needle that can be bought at local pharmacies. They do require subscriptions, though."

Travis tensed. "How sure did she sound?"

I shrugged. "Very sure. Why?"

"You asked me to get the file on her father's death. Betty's father was a diabetic. That was the cause of death on the certificate. His sugar was so low his heart just stopped, died in his sleep."

"She and I haven't talked about him, but she didn't mention that to me."

My father stared into the fire, methodically stroking his silver goatee. "Matilda and Betty were very unhappy in that house, Antonia. Richard was a cruel and arrogant man."

"I ran inquiries on Richard Renkin, Sr. and Nathan Mesters. I didn't get much information on Mesters, but at least a hundred references on Renkin. Businessman of the Year, yada, yada, yada. Made Sister Theresa look like an average woman, and we know that isn't true." I sighed. "Can't believe everything we find on the Internet."

"He made an advance on your mother at the church fair when we first moved to this town. She was so furious, she called him every name she could think of in Cajun and French. Caused quite a scene, actually."

"I don't remember that, Papa. What happened after she put him in his place?"

"He apologized to her and everyone else, explaining that it was all a misunderstanding. When I saw the crowd growing around the food pavilion, I picked you up in my arms and got over there, just in time to hear her call him a "filthy pig" though he didn't know what she said."

I searched my brain for any recollection of that particular fair, but I'd attended so many they were all a shifting collage of memories. "Did Matilda know?"

He looked at me now. "She knew. She came out of the tent and walked around the wooden table and slapped his face. Then she linked arms with your mother and they went back into the makeshift kitchen. The women quietly went on with cooking the corn and pig and greens while the men gathered around Richard, slapping his back and laughing."

"We watched all that and I don't remember anything at all. Amazing."

"After Matilda slapped Richard, I sent you off to play with Betty and the other children. Your mother was always the stronger of us, my pet. I wanted to challenge him there in front of his low-class cronies, but your mother forbid me to do so. She did not want any more embarrassment for Matilda. She considered Matilda her friend."

The phone rang and I started to get up, but Travis's arms held me securely. A moment later, his cell phone vibrated, and he let me go.

"Buchanan," he answered. A second later, I was unceremoniously dumped on the floor in front of the sofa as he jumped to his feet.

"The damned garage is on fire!"

## CHAPTER EIGHT

We dashed out of the house like the Keystone cops.

"Grab the hose, let's see if we can slow it down," Travis yelled as he ran toward the fire with the extinguisher from the kitchen. "Aim the water at the base of the fire," he shouted over his shoulder.

Orange, red, and purple flames danced above the roofline at the back of the garage and judging by the smoke rolling around the front of the building, the far side must have been burning pretty well too. A seventy-five-year-old structure provided a lot of usable fuel for a fire. I was thankful the building was a good distance from the house and across the street from our nearest neighbor.

I could hear sirens off in the distance and prayed they were heading our way. My father unraveled the hose as I ran toward the garage, but I'd lost sight of Travis.

"Papa, get the truck out of the driveway-the keys are on the hook by the back door."

"Travis," I yelled over the crackling and low hiss of the fire, as I reached the rear of the garage. My eyes filled with tears from the smoke. My heart was jammed in my throat, my hands shook so bad I fumbled with the nozzle and dropped the hose twice. I heard gravel fly as Papa backed the truck into the street.

The sirens grew louder as I aimed the powerful stream of water at the base of the wall and concentrated on a prayer to keep my husband safe. I heard glass breaking and dropped to the ground, fearing an explosion.

"AJ," Travis shouted from somewhere on the North side of the garage, "get the water on the garage door! I'm going to release it and get the car out!"

Scrambling to my feet, I dragged the hose to the front of the building and aimed it at the door. The flashing red lights of the fire trucks added to the smoke for an eerie scene.

"Just get out, Travis. Leave the car. Just get out of there!" I screamed.

A firefighter grabbed my arms and pulled me away from the driveway. "There's someone in there?" he asked.

"My husband. He's trying to get my car out before it blows up."

"You get over by the house and stay there. If he opens that door, an explosion is almost a guarantee." He motioned to the other firefighters to follow him, and I dragged my leaden feet in the direction of my father.

I gripped his hand. "Where the hell is he, Papa?"

"I don't know, Antonia. I'm sure he will be okay."

We watched in silence as the wide water hoses expanded like bloated boa constrictors and blasted the fire with a thousand gallons of water per minute.

"Breathe, Antonia. Your Travis will be fine," my father said, swiping at a tear I didn't even feel rolling down my cheek. "The fire is almost out, see?"

"Then where is he?" I felt an all too familiar tightness in my chest, like my heart and lungs were being squeezed by a powerful fist.

"Are you all right, dear?" asked a woman from beside me. I'd been so focused on the garage that I didn't see Mrs. Gardener approach us.

I nodded. "Was it you that called Travis?"

"My Daniel did. We were going to take Buddy for a walk and when we came out the front door, we noticed the fire on the other side of the garage. I'm so sorry."

"Well, thank you, Mrs. Gardener. Thank you for calling the fire department, too."

She stood to the side of us and watched the men work around the garage. I dropped my dad's hand and headed for the garage.

"Antonia…" my father called to my back. I waved at him. I was going to find my husband.

"Miss, you'll have to wait…"

I shook myself free of the fireman's grasp on my left arm. "I want to know where my husband is and I'm not waiting any longer to find out."

I heard the garage door open and began to run toward the driveway. Two large men in yellow jackets and massive black boots stopped me.

"We've got your husband out front. The paramedics are working on him."

"I want to see him," I growled, wrestling myself free. A look that worried me passed between the two men. I'd seen it before, the night Rick was shot to death. "Where is he?"

The younger man motioned for me to follow him. I took in a deep breath of acrid air, squared my shoulders, and marched alongside the firefighter. We stopped at the back of the paramedic wagon, where Travis was laying on the gurney. I started to cry when I saw his feeble wave in my direction.

"What in the world were you thinking, Travis?"

An oxygen mask covered his nose and mouth, a large, blood-soaked bandage adorned his left temple, and a paramedic had a blood pressure cuff on his right arm. I took his left hand in both of mine and held tight.

The first aid squad truck appeared in the driveway, lights flashing, but no siren. Half the town seemed to be on my front lawn, and I wished I had my camera. Someone started that fire, and I was betting the arsonist was still present. I scanned the faces, but all were familiar. *This can't be someone I know, can it?*

Someone placed their hands on my shoulders from behind me. I turned to see Deputy Shane Davis, in civilian clothes.

"Are you all right?" he asked Travis while wrapping a tired, navy blue blanket around my shoulders.

"No, he isn't…" I swung around to face Travis. The oxygen mask was replaced with a thin, transparent hose. He was a mess, the smoke and soot streaked across his cheeks and chin where the mask had been.

"So, why in the world did you go in there?" I hissed.

"You and Rick built that car. I wanted to save it for you."

"That damned car doesn't mean more to me than you do, Travis Buchanan. You had no right to risk your life for that car."

"I thought I could do it…I miscalculated, that's all."

"I'll say. Gee, another headline for the local paper. Hell, at this rate, nothing else in the entire county will get reported. Want news? Just check on that crazy Buchanan clan over in Chastity Creek. More laughs than a pond full of gators."

While he laughed, I started to cry. And shake, and then the first aid crew put him in the wagon, Shane Davis climbed aboard and off they went. And I stood there, watching the people wander away. My father walked me back into the house.

I collapsed in the pew at the kitchen table while my father made a pot of coffee and the deputy, and the fire captain reviewed statements. My father put the bottle of Jack Daniel's on the table with four glasses, pouring one for him and one for me. The fire officials that were filling the room were on their own.

\*\*\*

When I arrived at the hospital, Travis was still in the radiology department getting a CT scan of his head. I went looking for a cup of coffee, which turned out to be a horrible idea. I thought about the coffee at Quantico that was made three times a day, black and strong enough to remove tarnish from the Washington monument. The coffee in the woman's shelter had been just a bit weaker, but much more pleasurable.

"Mrs. Buchanan?"

"Yes," I answered the doctor who stood in the doorway.

"We're going to keep your husband over night. He wants to see you. If you'll follow me, I'll take you to him."

I trailed behind his billowing white coat as he hustled us through the quiet hallways, dodging medication carts and stacked dinner trays that still waited to be collected.

At room 302, he stopped and waved me ahead of him. He pulled back the privacy curtain and my knees all but buckled.

"Well, you do look better than the garage, Crimestopper. Not much, though."

He smiled, but obviously laughing was too painful. His right eye was turning bright purplish-red, his brow was steri-stripped, and he had a jagged gash in his forehead, right at the hairline. He patted the edge of the hospital bed and I sat beside him.

"We're going to keep you for observation tonight," the doctor said, looking at Travis. "You have a confirmed concussion and a hairline fracture in the left clavicle. We'll give you something to ease the headache, but we're going to put you on a monitor. Your lungs are pretty much clear, so apparently you were not directly inside the fire zone." He smiled at us both, turned on his heel and disappeared through the open doorway.

"Then you weren't inside the garage? Why the hell didn't you answer me when I was screaming for you?" The trembling was back, and I got up off the bed to pace. I stared at the green and white floor tiles while I waited for his answer.

"I was going in the garage. Since the fire was on the back side, or so I thought, I went around to the other side, figured I'd get in through the window, release the door, and get the car out. Someone whacked me with something before I got the window open all the way."

"Did you see who it was by any chance?" I asked.

"Sorry, honey, I didn't. Heard something behind me and turned in time to get smacked in the face. Big. That's only an impression, but he was big. Could have been a black bear for all I know."

I sighed and collapsed in the side chair by the bed. "Okay, we've got big and male. Bobby Joe big, I wonder?"

"Yeah, that sort of big, but I couldn't tell you if it was him or not."

"I guess that's a start. The fire chief confirmed the fire was arson. Accelerant was gasoline. Not very creative, but effective. Especially on a building that old."

"I'm sorry about the car, honey."

I took his hand in mine and forced him to look at me. By the look on his face, it was painful to keep his eyes open. "The Shark was a classic. It was special to me because along with all that fiberglass work and engine work and the paychecks it consumed, someone I loved very much helped me make that dream come true.

"But nothing in this world, not even that car, means more to me than you, Mr. Buchanan. Thank you for trying to save her, but don't ever do anything like that again. Promise?"

He didn't acknowledge my request. "Did anyone else get hurt? Did the firefighters get the fire out before it spread? They were here forever taking statements, but they weren't giving out any information."

I put my head down on his chest and listened to his steady heartbeat. "You, the garage, and the car, were the only casualties. And thanks to the new city water system, there was enough water in the fire hydrant to keep the block from burning down. All's well that ends well."

He wrapped his good arm around my shoulder and stroked my hair. "The soot really did a lot for your spikes," he joked, tugging on the strands of short hair that probably now stood straight up on my head.

"Thanks. A new look – maybe I'll keep it," I laughed back. And then I started to cry, again, probably more out of relief than anything else. To bury one husband you love is hard enough, but to have to bury two would be more than I had the strength to do.

He tightened his grip on me and held me until my emotions had drained to a sniffle. I scrubbed my blotchy cheeks with a handful of stiff, hospital tissues and the nurse came in to check all of his monitors and numbers.

When the nurse had him comfortable and he'd gone to sleep, I stayed at the window a long time, watching the beam from the lighthouse splash illumination on the Matanzas River.

Was the fire tied to Matilda's death, the Donovan trial or something else all together? A threat, a warning, or revenge?

# CHAPTER NINE

In the quiet of the night, the soft clicking and buzzing of the machines that monitored my husband's condition soothed my aching brain. Even my own breathing was closer to being normal after a couple of hours. The tightness in my chest was no better, though.

I got up and walked to the window and looked out over a sleeping St. Augustine and the river that divided the mainland from the island. I saw the lights of a sailboat drift along on the water, the boat unseen in the darkness. I returned to the wooden-armed chair beside Travis's bed. At some point, I slept.

"Antonia?" someone whispered, startling me awake from my crooked perch.

I winced as I looked into the face of Deputy Davis. Glancing at Travis who still slept, I motioned Shane to join me in the hall. He carried a bag from Everything Bagel, one of the few eateries open before dawn.

"You are a wonderful man, Deputy." We sat in the chairs at the end of the hallway, under a bank of windows and the auspices of a forty-foot-tall palm tree. He handed me tiny creamers, sugar packets and a thin brown stirrer along with a cup of steaming coffee. "Thank you for staying with my father, last night."

"My pleasure. My wife brought us breakfast this morning. There's also a patrol car in the area to discourage any more visitors."

"I sure wish I could figure out where this latest attack came from," I muttered, stirring my coffee and flexing my shoulders.

"There have been others?" he asked, trying to keep his voice low. I told him about my psycho poet and he shook his head, as he pulled a small notebook from his jacket pocket. "Anything else?"

"Travis and I aren't exactly popular with the Fletcher-Donovan clan, as you can imagine. They believe Margie killed her husband in cold blood, not self-defense."

"What aren't you telling me?" he prodded after another swig of coffee.

I didn't talk about Rick's death to many people. The burden was still too heavy, the guilt too easily renewed. I shrugged.

"Nothing that would impact this case, I'm sure."

65

"AJ, you know yourself, life isn't cut and dried, and neither is murder. If there's something in your pasts that could be bringing this down on Chastity Creek now, you need to tell me about it."

"I just don't think it's relevant. I'd tell you if I thought it was."

He picked up his coffee and sat back in the chair, stretching long legs out in front of him. "Okay, so maybe you tell me so you can shed some of that weight on your shoulders."

I looked at him. "You know Deputy, I'll bet we could be friends. LEO's don't have many friends that aren't in the same business."

"That's for true. But you guys have been there, and you know what they say."

I laughed. "Once a cop, always a cop."

He leaned forward, resting his elbows on his knees. "So, what mystery from your past is still unsolved? That night at the mill, Travis mentioned Washington...."

I shook my head. He was right. *What if the danger had followed me from D.C.? Did I have a right not to tell him?*

"My first husband Rick was killed on a DEA raid, and it wasn't a friendly-fire accident like the agency claimed it was."

"You were FBI and he was DEA? Must have been some home life you two had."

I couldn't help but smile. "We had our challenges, that's for sure. He was an agent though. I was a forensic photographer. I didn't do investigation work, really. Sure, I was on scene to take photographs sometimes, but most of my work was in the lab. I had all the basic training and found I liked the martial arts and guns, but never acquired much taste for the boring, wait-around-for-something-to-happen part. After Rick died, it wasn't too hard a decision to leave it behind."

"You said his death wasn't an accident."

"He'd been edgy and worried about the mission coming up. He was taking me to the gun range to practice more and he insisted on checking insurance policies, doing a will, all the end-of-life activities. All he would tell me was that the deal going down that Friday morning was more about an internal investigation than the drug bust."

"He didn't survive the raid?"

I cleared my throat, gulped my coffee, and nodded. "I was a wreck and although we always respected each other's confidentiality issues, he'd never been so spooked before. I tailed him, circled back, and parked about two blocks from the action. I had my camera of course and was taking pictures of the area when the first gun blast went off. I hit the ground, crawled up to see through the hedge. By the time the smoke cleared, he was dead. Oddly enough, he and the suspected dealer were the only casualties."

"I haven't known you very long, but I suspect you didn't leave DC quietly. Bet they were madder than hornets when you got done."

"True and I didn't really accomplish anything. But, I have a reporter friend at the Post who still thinks it needs to be resolved. Maybe someone else does too."

"What's the reporter's name?" he asked, pencil poised.

"Actually, he's now the senior managing editor. Joe Flynn."

"I gotta tell you," he said. "I don't like any of this. I asked the local lab to run the plastic cap Betty found. No prints on it. There was trace solution inside, however. The syringe was loaded, capped and carried there. They'll identify what the syringe dispensed."

"Did the M.E. do toxicology on Matilda's body?" I asked.

"Yes, that's standard operating procedure, but it could be weeks before we get any information. Those tests are run at the state lab."

We sat quiet and drank coffee for a few minutes, then he leaned toward me, speaking barely above a whisper.

"I asked the Sheriff to approve another look at Matilda's body. I know we're not sure if the needle cap is even related to her death, but I want them to go over her for punctures that can't be explained. We weren't looking for anything like that, so maybe it's there and we missed it."

"Like I've said before, I like the way you think, Deputy Davis. Betty will be okay if you can't release the body right away. She's still working on the arrangements with the church."

"The Sheriff approved the request last night and coroner will review today. Betty can have her mother picked up by the mortuary tomorrow. Most of them work Saturdays. That way if she wants to do the funeral early next week, the funeral home will have enough time."

My cell phone vibrated on my hip. I glanced down, pulled it free and flipped it open. "Good morning, Betty," I said, looking at the deputy.

I listened to her as she explained that the fire had been on the morning news and how upset she was about the whole thing. Was everyone all right? Was the house okay? How was Travis this morning? I answered as quickly as I could for being mentally asleep despite the caffeine. She finally fell silent.

"I'll be home as soon as they release Travis, which should be some time this morning. Going to work from home today, so call the house if you need me," I told her.

Snapping the phone closed, I held it in my hand as though it contained all the answers to my universe. Shane Davis stood beside me, looking out the windows at the beautiful blue sky. Claustrophobia began to gnaw at me.

"Mrs. Buchanan?" asked a nurse from the station a few yards away. I looked up.

"Doctor Remmy is going to release your husband now. There are two television trucks in the main parking lot and several calls have come in asking about Mr. Buchanan, so I assume the media interest and your husband are connected."

I stifled a groan. Of course, the area would be interested in how the attorney of an alleged husband-killer had ended up in the hospital and what affect if any, that would have on Margie's trial.

"I'll talk to you later, Shane. Let me get him out of here and home where we can both relax. If I'm really lucky, perhaps my father has completed programming the security system and we'll sleep safe and sound tonight."

Davis nodded. "He worked on it almost non-stop. I don't think he went to bed until after two this morning."

We walked through the doorway to Travis' room in time to see him disappear into the bathroom. I pulled his clean clothes from the backpack I'd brought with me last night.

"I'm back on duty on the four-to-four tonight, so if you can't reach me, call the SO. For all our sakes, I'm hoping you have a very quiet day." With a smile, he turned and left me to wait for my battered husband to finish his shower.

I called my father. "Everything okay, Papa?"

"Joe Flynn called. He would like you to call him back."

"That's just terrific. He'll have to wait. We'll be heading home soon; do you need anything?"

"I need my daughter to be safe and happy and whole. This Flynn is connected with your Rick, yes?" he prodded.

"Yes, I haven't talked to him in over a year, but he doesn't call me to chat, so I'm sure he needs something. I just don't have enough to give him anything right now."

"If you were not my daughter, I would advise you to just leave these things alone. However, you are like your mother, and I would be wasting my time."

My laugh was hoarse but heartfelt. "You are just as stubborn in your own way as Mama was."

His chuckle kept the smile on my face. "That is true, I suppose. When will I see you?"

"We're on our way shortly. Please keep the house locked and if you see anything you don't like, you call the number on the refrigerator door, okay?"

\*\*\*

My father met us at the back porch steps, his brow furrowed, his eyes dark with concern. "So, how do you feel?" he asked Travis.

"I've got a whopper of a headache, but otherwise I'm doing just fine. You got a lot done," Travis pointed out, glancing at the security cameras installed on the west side of the house.

Papa straightened a little and flashed us a toothy smile. "That nice deputy helped me with the ladder early this morning. As soon as we had light, we were out here. Today I'll get the solar collector hooked up and then we'll test some of this."

I shook my head and went into the house with an armload of items from the hospital and a bag of dressings and prescriptions from the hospital pharmacy. I spotted the message light blinking on our answering machine. Did I dare hit the "play" button?

*Whatever.* I pressed the button and poured myself a glass of orange juice. The first call was from Travis's new secretary Summer Whitestone, sending her best wishes and instructions to call her if we needed anything. The second was Kathy from the Café.

"AJ, I just wanted to check on you two and see if everyone is all right. Lon said to tell you not to worry about the 'Vette, he'll help you get it fixed up in no time. Call me if you need anything and come on down for dinner tonight."

Well, at least the only messages were friendly ones. Of course, did we dare venture into Half Pot Café without fear of getting the place torched or blown up? I wasn't real sure.

"What's on your agenda the rest of the afternoon, Trouble?" my husband asked as he ruffled my filthy hair.

"First thing is a long, hot shower. Maybe a nap. I have to get the Burlington case file emailed to Interstate Insurance, and then I'm all yours."

He grabbed the back of my flannel shirt and pulled me against him. "You're all mine right now," he breathed in my ear.

How can you argue with a man when he's right? I turned to give him a kiss and realized he looked as tired as I felt.

I smiled. "Your head's making promises your body can't keep, honey. Go upstairs and lay down. I'll join you after my shower."

He winked one purplish-black eye and I flinched. The man was just about unstoppable. I hoped we could keep it that way.

\*\*\*

When I woke at three, sunlight peaked through the blinds and the house was silent. Travis was asleep, so I eased out of bed, pulled on jeans, a sweatshirt, and heavy wool socks.

I looked into the spare room on my way down the hall where Papa was sleeping, too. Slipping down the stairs, I headed for my office and started the computer.

System started up and coffee brewing, I checked out some of my dad's handiwork. Compact, motion activated cameras now adorned our white crown moldings in all of the first-floor rooms. I wandered to the window to take a closer look at the window catch which sported a tiny antenna. We were wireless, indeed.

I poured a cup of coffee and took it to my desk. Just as surely as I knew in my gut that my late husband's death hadn't been accidental, I now knew Matilda's wasn't either. And that meant there was a killer close by.

While the background reports and news clips piled into my in-box on Betty's brother, I finished the last of my open insurance case files and emailed it to the secured server.

"Intruder Alert!" a shrill voice announced from somewhere behind me. I dropped to the floor, reached to the desktop for my .38 and crab-crawled to the back side of the desk.

The shrill voice stopped, but heavy, hurried footsteps, didn't.

## CHAPTER TEN

My heart pounded and my mouth went dry. Footsteps hurried in my direction. Just as I was wondering if I had the courage to jump out at my attacker, the shrill voice sounded again.

"Antonia," my father called. "Everything is okay. The system needs some fine tuning, that's all."

I peered around the desk, lowering my gun. "Papa, you have got to do something about that voice. That will make me crazy."

He smiled at me. "That was the alarm mode. I forgot to put the system to sleep when we rested this afternoon. I'm sorry to have scared you like that."

I got to my feet, placing my gun back on the desk. "Scared doesn't cover it, Papa. Thank God I didn't shoot before you called to me."

He waved me off, turning to leave the room. "You knew Travis and I were here; you would never shoot without knowing who or what you were shooting."

"Glad you're so sure about that," I muttered, following him into the kitchen.

"What the hell is going on?" Travis moaned, leaning against the doorframe in his Seminole lounge pants with his Glock in his hand.

I nodded to my father to explain. "Asta detected motion at an egress and put out an alert. I'll have to find out which door or window trip malfunctioned."

Travis put his gun on top of the refrigerator and sat down at the table next to me. "Is this going to be our new normal, Trouble?"

"Hey, you wanted the alarm system, fella. You and the geriatric rebel here thought this was a great idea. There's bound to be some kinks to work out. Hell, I think I almost had a heart attack."

"I'm sorry, my children. I will work on it tonight. Why don't you go get some dinner and relax a little? All the excitement is too much for us all, I think, no?"

"I think, yes. We could go over to the Half Pot for some dinner, if you're up to it," I said, looking at Travis.

"I'll be okay with a shower. Besides, we could learn a lot over there–the place is gossip central." He stood to go upstairs but turned to my father first. "Henri, Asta is quite a remarkable system. I appreciate all the work you've done for us here."

My father's eyes danced with delight. "You're welcome. And I will have this fixed before we retire for the night. You two go out. I'll fix a salad and get back to work."

Both men left me sitting at the table alone. It was nearly five o'clock and dusk had settled in. In two weeks, people around the country would be celebrating Thanksgiving. I glanced out the window at the burned frame that yesterday morning was our garage.

I had *much* to be thankful for.

***

We pulled in around the corner and into the restaurant parking lot, just around seven. After locking the truck, we let ourselves in through the back door and wound our way through the kitchen.

In the twenties, so the stories go, this was the route the mayor and police chief used to exit the establishment from time to time, undoubtedly, to make sure their wives never caught them leaving the warm beds of the working girls they visited several nights a week. A lot of colorful history attached to a former brothel, including the fact that it was run by the town father's daughter, Chastity.

The Half Pot got its name from the fact that when Kathy and Lon bought the place, the water was delivered by a pump from a shallow well. The pressure was so low that it was impossible to brew more than a half pot of coffee at a time. That was ten years ago, and the newer town water system rectified the issue, but they kept the name, anyway.

We slid into the last booth on the right, though Travis's slide was a bit slower than mine. Just like Earp or Dillon, we could see all the exits. I waved to Kathy, so she'd know we were there. She waved back, balancing three steaming plates on her left arm.

Travis pointed to the old photo tucked in a battered black frame on the wall behind my head. "That's old man Renkin in that publicity picture. Taken the week his foreman was fired, I believe."

"And how would you know that?"

"You're not the only trained investigator in the family, you know. It's a photo that several area papers ran, including the St. Augustine Record and the Palatka Daily News."

Kathy stopped by, wiping her hands on her apron before whipping out her pad and badly-chewed pencil. "What would you two warriors like?"

I winked at her. "Chicken fried steak, smashed potatoes, and greens."

"And you, Perry Mason?" she asked looking around as the bells over the front door rang again.

"Chef's salad for me. We'll get iced teas from the cooler."

"You two in a hurry?" she asked, stuffing the pad back into the front apron pocket.

We both answered "No."

"Good, maybe Lon and I can join you in a few minutes. It's quiet for a Friday night." She disappeared through the swinging doors to the kitchen.

Travis got out of the seat, despite my protests, and sauntered toward the cooler. He moved sort of sleek and powerful like a panther and I loved watching him, I just hated getting caught at it. The bandage over his right temple and discolored eye just made him seem all the more dangerous. My very own battered pirate prince.

Lon and Kathy appeared with our dinners and coffee for themselves, and before long we were enjoying great food and rare time with hard-working friends.

"We're so glad that you two weren't badly hurt in that fire. We held our breath for hours waiting for someone to tell us who went roaring out of here in the ambulance," Kathy said, her eyes filling with tears.

Lon nodded. "That Deputy Davis dropped by to let us know you were all right." He pointed at the bandage that edged Travis's temple. "Do you have any idea who hit you?"

Laughing, Travis shrugged. "No idea at all. I am surprised that you knew I was hit, though. I'd have kept that under wraps if I were investigating this thing."

"The town's total population is nine hundred fifty people, Travis. How do you keep that quiet? Your neighbor heard what you said to the First Aid guys. She called everyone to be on the lookout for someone running around with a two by four."

Visualizing a Dick Dastardly-type villain armed with a long hunk of pine, we all laughed for minutes, ignoring the pointed stares of the other patrons.

Kathy reached over and touched the back of Travis's hand. "We know you can't discuss the murder trial, but we wanted to tell you we're all for what you're doing."

"I'm just doing my job. The woman needed a defense attorney, and I was available."

"Paper says you're doing it pro bono. I didn't think attorneys took cases they didn't get paid for anymore."

Travis shrugged. "If I hadn't requested it, the judge would have assigned someone from the public defender's office. It doesn't hurt once in a while to help someone out and this was important. To me and to AJ."

Lon lifted his mug in the air as a salute. "Well, we're very thankful she's got you fighting for her. Good luck."

As we ate and Kathy filled us in on all the town gossip we'd missed by not dropping in during the past week, I shifted the conversation to the Renkin family. Because my family didn't run with the same crowd, I still had a lot to learn about the relationships in that household.

"I think I remember something about Matilda having a sister. I'm not sure though. Should be someone in town that could tell us." Kathy looked around the room. Only four people remained now that it was past nine o'clock. "You can ask Darlene over there. She might remember her. Is it important?"

"I have no idea, but it's a puzzle piece I didn't have before. Can't hurt to run it down, right?"

Kathy walked with me to the seventyish woman seated near the window and introduced me. We chatted for a few minutes, then returned to our table.

"Well?" prodded Travis.

"Matilda had a sister who was apparently sent to a boarding school after their mother died. Miss Darlene thought the name was Dora or Donna or something like that – couldn't remember for sure. Older than Matilda. That's all she remembers."

We stood to say our goodbyes. I gave Kathy a hug. "That's more than I had a few minutes ago. Thanks a ton for all your support. If you think of someone else who might know more, let me know."

"Sure will," she said, patting my shoulder.

I was quiet as we climbed into the truck to go home.

In the morning, I'd call Betty. Why hadn't she ever mentioned her aunt? And why didn't I remember her having one?

## CHAPTER ELEVEN

After a quiet, uneventful evening at the Buchanan casa, the cool, clear morning seemed particularly invigorating. I ran the three miles to the river and back before Travis was even awake. The morning mist mingled with the scents of recently tilled soil and I took extra deep breaths along the way.

Entry to our Victorian home now required my thumbprint. Since that didn't unlock the door the way it was supposed to, my father had to let me in. Obviously, our state-of-the-art security system still needed some work.

"You shouldn't be out alone, Antonia. Someone is looking to hurt you. Why make it so easy?" he chided as he pushed a glass of juice in front of me. I didn't reply.

"The oranges on your trees need to be picked and enjoyed. They are falling off. They will be over-ripe in a few more days. You could do those things instead of poking a stick in the snake pit every day," he continued.

I drank dutifully, placed the glass in the sink, and offered him a cheeky smile. "Feel free to pick the fruit, Papa. You'll enjoy it much more than I would." I winked at him. "I'll get a shower and start some breakfast. Don't worry so much, okay? I didn't take my usual route today just in case someone's watching, but I wanted to see who was hanging around in Veteran's Park early in the morning."

Without waiting for his retort, I climbed the stairs two at a time, took a quick shower, and was dressed and almost done mixing my buttermilk pancakes when Travis appeared in the kitchen. My father had disappeared into the living room to watch CNN.

"How you feeling this morning?" I asked, pouring a mug of coffee and setting it in front of him at the counter.

"Not too bad, considering. Headache is bearable. The rest of me feels like I was kicked by a mule but guess that's to be expected."

"You coughed on and off all night. I was afraid you weren't sleeping at all."

He shrugged. "I slept, Trouble. Don't make a big deal about this, okay?"

I returned the shrug. I could give as good as I got. "Sure. Same goes for you, fella."

I sprinkled water on the griddle and watched it sizzle as though it was a unique scientific experiment. I poured the pancake batter onto the hot surface, savoring the smell of vanilla and buttermilk that filled the air.

"What's on your agenda today, Mrs. Buchanan?" Travis asked.

"I need to talk to Betty. I don't know if she's going to be in the area or not, but I'll call her after breakfast and find out. Maybe look around and see who I can find among our homeless population that might be able to help me. And I need to get the rental car handled." I put a plate in front of Travis and motioned for him to eat. "How about you? You still plan on seeing the judge on Monday?"

He nodded. "And I have a lot of work to finish up, so I'll be in my office most of the day."

"Can you work from here or are you going into Palatka?"

"I'll have to go to the office. I called Summer before I came downstairs. She'll meet me there around noon. In the meantime, I'm going to clean up and visit Margie at the jail. I still have a couple of questions for her."

I called my father to join us for breakfast, then sat down with my own. "What's bothering you, Travis? That gut of yours telling you something's not right? Did I miss something?"

He reached over and covered my hand with his. "I just have a couple of questions I want the answers to before the judge asks the questions, that's all. The timeline is niggling at me. I need to be clear about why Margie waited almost an hour to call 911."

"She wanted to make sure he was dead, probably," I said, recalling the women in D.C. who'd told me stories about abusive partners that would curl a Marine's hair.

"While I understand, let's hope that's not the answer, honey." He finished his breakfast, stood, and put his dish in the sink. "And, if it is, it's better that I know it going in."

"Well, as long as you don't need me, I'm gonna snoop around the Palatka waterfront, see if anyone can identify my homeless guy. There's a small colony of homeless vets down that way. I ran along the outskirts of the park, but I didn't see him this morning."

"I don't want you going anywhere alone, AJ."

"You sound like my father," I growled, pushing away my plate.

My father appeared on cue. "What is wrong with that? Wanting you to be safe makes us both intelligent men, I think. And maybe you—too arrogant?"

I sent him a look that would peel paint off a clapboard house. "Eat your breakfast before it's totally cold. I've got calls to make."

Like the mature thirty-nine-year-old woman that I am, I did not stick my tongue out at either of them before I slammed my office door.

***

Travis was long gone when Betty arrived at the house just before one o'clock. The usually azure blue skies were cloud-covered, dark and grayish, a cold front on its way across the Florida peninsula. I pulled on a heavy hooded sweatshirt with the FBI logo on the back, snapped the Smith and Wesson on my belt, and grabbed my backpack.

"AJ?" she called through the screen door on the back porch.

"Betty Renkin," my father called out, coming out from under the kitchen cabinet where he was rewiring Asta for something or other. "Come in, dear."

I walked into the kitchen to find Betty and my father in a New Orlean's style greeting. Kissing the air on either side of their respective cheeks, they held each other at arm's length.

"I am so sorry about your mother, Betty."

"Thank you, sir. And I'm sorry about your trouble, too. I'm sure AJ and Travis are happy to have you here, though."

"I'm lucky they are such good people. And my Antonia will help you. She is your friend."

The smile faded from Betty's face. "She's a good person, that's for sure." She dropped her hands to her side and flashed me a pale smile. "Your chariot awaits you," she quipped, sweeping her right arm before her as she bowed at the waist.

"Yeah, well we can pick up a rental car at Enterprise on the way back, maybe. They didn't have any this morning." I turned to my father.

"Please lock up after I go. I'll call you and check in, okay? I should be back around four at the latest." With a kiss to his cheek, Betty and I fled out the door and dove into her Mustang.

"How're things with Michael?" I asked when we reached SR17.

"Better. He's much more civil. Actually, we're coming down tomorrow so we can talk to the minister after church. Thought we'd attend service and then set up the final arrangements for the funeral. Going to be on Monday if we can arrange it. Master's is picking up my mom's body this morning. Can you come on Monday? It'll be small. The paper's going to run one small announcement tomorrow. According to the funeral home records, she wanted a cremation and church service, no visitation."

We were approaching the top of Veteran's Memorial Bridge and I looked out the window at the St. John's River. The steam from the Seminole Energy Company stacks drifted lazily northward in the gentle breeze. "Sounds like your mother, taking care of every detail, right? We'll be there. Do you need us to do anything?"

"Just be there, okay? And help me figure out what's going on."

"Yes ma'am. Let's see who we can find hanging out, okay?"

Betty turned left onto 9th Street and wheeled the sports car easily along Main Street to the river. Even though the day was calm and almost sixty-five degrees, only a half-dozen pickup trucks with boat trailers were in the lot. We drove past the public pier and parked near the restroom building.

We spotted two street people playing cards at a sheltered picnic table, so we each put a bottle of water in one pocket and some granola bars in the other.

White egrets stretched their long black legs as they walked along the river shoreline, ignoring us as we approached. The shrimp were starting to run and they would not be distracted from what would be a plentiful meal. We approached the table, scuffing our feet so we didn't startle our intended targets.

"Hello, sirs," I called out. "Would you be willing to talk to us for a few minutes?"

With the sun behind us heading for the western horizon on the St. John's River, the slighter of the two squinted up at us. We knelt on the ground in front of them. Betty placed a bottle of water and three granola bars on the bench between the two men. I followed her lead.

"What can we do for you ladies?" the taller man asked, pulling his tattered coat closer to his chest to protect against the wind.

I pulled out a picture of Matilda and showed it to the pair. "Maybe you've seen this woman in the past week or so?" I asked.

They looked carefully, the taller man holding the picture almost at the end of his nose so that he could see it. They both shook their heads.

"Don't look like no street lady, to me," the shorter fellow said through broken teeth. "What did she do?"

Betty looked away a moment, then took the picture back. "She died."

"Was her mama, George," said tall man softly. "Looks just like this little lady, here."

"I'm sorry, honey," he said. "Me and George here a lot of the time. Never seen this lady, though."

"Did you see anything unusual last Friday night, maybe?" I asked. "Or maybe, you've seen this guy?" I handed them my partial photo of the man who surprised me at the mill.

They laughed, a rusty sound part-gurgle, part cough. "Lots of 'unusual' going on from your point of view. Nothing unusual from ours."

"James ain't lying. After dark, all sorts of people come out and hang down here. You think this guy involved in this?" George asked me.

"I don't know what to think. Someone picked this lady up at her home and drove her to where she was found, just up the river." I waved to the northeast shoreline. "I came across someone who seemed to be living in the old Renkin paper mill. I don't think he's involved in her death, but he might have seen something."

George held the enlarged photo and studied it carefully. "This might be Sarge, but the picture ain't too good."

I nodded in agreement. "He wasn't interested in posing for portraits, that's for sure. Is Sarge a regular around here?"

James smiled, a toothless grin full of mischief. "He's a ninja. He's here, sometimes he's not. He's still in the Vietnam jungle if you get my meanin', so he needs to be alone sometimes."

"Any idea where he goes?"

They both shook their heads. We thanked them for their time and walked along the river walk, back to the car.

"Now what?" Betty asked.

"Hell if I know. I could stake out the mill and see if this guy shows up again, but I don't know if that's worth the time it will take. Travis helps some of these guys, so now that we suspect he's a veteran, maybe he'll remember something. And we can stop by the church kitchens and shelters, show the picture around. Make some donations. Somebody must know this guy."

We drove to Travis's office and parked the Mustang in his lot. Summer buzzed us into the office.

"Mrs. Buchanan, how are you?" she asked in her soft, southern drawl.

Blonde and blue-eyed, she was the single mother of twin boys who were her spitting image. I liked her but I wished Travis had hired a sixty-something with a million grandkids instead.

"I'm doing fine. How is Travis holding up?"

"He's still at the jail. He should be here soon, though. Do you want to wait for him?"

I shook my head. "We're going to walk around town, talk to some people. We parked Betty's car in the lot out back, okay?" I turned toward the door, then stopped. "Oh, maybe you can ask him to look at this picture. Maybe he's worked with this guy?"

"Sure. Stop in before you go home. I'm sure he'll be here by then."

"We'll do that, thanks," I said.

We stopped at the Presbyterian church hall and showed the photo.

"Sure looks like Sarge," the large woman said. "He was in here last week once or maybe twice. Haven't seen him since then, though."

I nodded. "Do you remember what day that was, maybe?"

"Nah. Everyday's pretty much the same. Might of been Tuesday or Wednesday. I'm sorry, I'm not sure."

"No, don't apologize. You've been a big help. If you see him again or if you think of anything else, maybe you could give me a call?" I handed her my business card.

"He is some kind of trouble? He's a pretty nice guy. Quiet and smart, too. Likes to play chess if he can find someone to play."

Betty smiled. "He's not in trouble, but he might be able to help us with something, that's all."

With several more locations to hit before we gave up, we moved on. The story was the same in all of them.

Betty and I walked twenty blocks and had donated a hundred dollars before we came back for the car. Most of the churches who helped out the homeless folks living in Palatka's back alleys and on the park benches had seen "Sarge" off and on but had no information about his current location. Sometimes, they said, he vanished for weeks.

Throughout the old city, which also serves as the county seat, historical events were captured in colorful murals painted on the sides of the old buildings.

On Third Street, Betty and I stopped to admire one of Palatka's recently restored murals. Billy Graham and the steamboats running up and down the St. John's River depicted a bit of Palatka's rich history, something that today's rundown buildings and vacant lots all but negated. The city was full of hopeful and hardworking people, though. A comeback was not beyond possibility.

When we got back to Travis's office, Summer had left, and he was locking up and getting ready to drive home.

"Successful day, I hope?" I asked as we walked toward Betty's car and his truck.

"Not a waste of time, anyway. I didn't recognize your fella from that photo, though. He's not someone that's come to see me." He glanced at the ground as though contemplating the fate of the world. "You checked the Methodist church, right? The guy that runs the kitchen there seems to know everyone."

"We did and Sarge was seen a couple of nights ago, but not since."

Travis gave me a quick kiss. "These guys have a lot of fears, real and imagined. He may surface again. We'll just have to hope for the best." With that, he tossed his briefcase into the truck, climbed gingerly into the cab, and waved as he drove away.

Betty eyed her watch. "Look, your rental won't be ready for another half hour, so let's hit Angels and have a shake. My treat."

"Sounds good to me."

We drove four blocks and pulled into a vacant drive-in lane. We placed our order with a waitress who no longer wore roller skates, but probably had more than her share of skating miles logged. We showed her the picture of our John Doe veteran, but aside from having seen him walk the highway a time or two, she didn't seem to know anything about him.

"Betty, do you have an Aunt Donna?"

She took a long pull on her lemonade and looked away from me. "I have an Aunt Dora. Short for Dorothea. She's my mother's half-sister. A little bit strange, always patting my hair and telling me how pretty I am, as though I was always three years old or something. My mother used to get very agitated when Dora was around, guess they didn't get along or something. I haven't seen her in years. Not since Uncle Nate's funeral."

"Will she be at the funeral?"

"I don't know. I left a message at the last phone number I had for her. She moved after Uncle Nate died. The last time I saw her was at his funeral."

"*Uncle* Nate?"

"Yeah, Aunt Dora was his wife. He was a good friend of my mother's. I think he worked for Father at one time. A really nice man, too. More of a father to me than *my* father ever was."

Our orders arrived and we hooked the trays over the car doors. I snagged an onion ring and nibbled at it, realizing how little I knew about Betty's childhood, other than what Matilda let us see.

"Richard Jr. must have been crushed by his father's death. Was he in Arizona by that time?"

She seemed to go a little pale, and I waited. She shook it off and forced a smile. "He was very upset. He was at the house the day Father died, I think. Some of that day is very fuzzy for me, even now."

"No word back from him yet?" I asked, washing down the rest of the fried treat with a gulp of thick, vanilla milk shake.

"Nope, his wife is still screening the calls, I think. She said she gave him my messages. I'm not calling again. He can go scratch."

She popped an onion ring in her mouth, chewed a minute or two, then swallowed. "You asked me to bring some photos with me. I have them in that folder." She pointed at the red file folder tucked in the door pocket. I pulled it out and opened it in my lap.

"That picture of Richard with the kids is from last Christmas. It was on Mom's bulletin board in the office."

My cell phone rang. I glanced at the display and then flipped it open. "Hi, Papa. How are you?"

I listened as he chided me for not checking in with him, which I had completely forgotten. "Well, Betty and I stopped at Angels. We're going to swing by the factory on the way home. I'll see you in an hour or so." He had interesting information, but I didn't want to discuss it in front of Betty, so it would have to wait.

"How's he doing?" she asked me.

"He's staying busy. The insurance company is giving him a hard time about paying for the repairs and of course, he's deeded the house to the college already, so this gets complicated. He's decided to resign his tenure in May. He's got a real problem with the attitude of most college students these days."

"Most students are ungrateful, self-absorbed young people totally unprepared for the real world or dealing with people in the proper manner. I know I was. It was all about me," Betty said.

"I guess. I was probably the same in my own way. I loved Georgetown, the people, the architecture, the night life, the diversity, all of it. And I was focused on being the very best photojournalist in the world. The idealism has dulled a bit, I think." I took the remaining onion ring and balled up the wax paper wrapper.

Betty slurped the last of her shake. "You think? I was so glad to get away from my father that I seldom even came home from school. I was an overachiever, too. I didn't want to disappoint my mother. She fought so hard to give me chances to be happy."

The waitress stopped by to pick up the trays and trash. "Let's go get your rental car, then I'm heading back to Orange Park, okay? Michael and I have to come back tomorrow, and I have to get his billable hours invoiced today."

"You know, I don't think I know what he does. Has his own company, you said?"

"He did very well in the early days of the dot com era, which is a good thing. And he invested well for the most part. Now he specializes in computer system security. Teaches companies how to beat the hackers at their own game."

Could Betty's husband be sending me the threatening email poetry that was so hard to trace? We pulled into the Enterprise car rental lot, but I was distracted.

"AJ, we're here. You going inside?"

I jumped, feeling guilty about the turn my thoughts had taken. "Sure." I collected the photos, my backpack, and my jacket. "Just let me make sure it's ready."

I ran inside the small building while Betty waited outside. Five minutes later I had a completed rental agreement, keys, and a bottle of spring water for the trip home.

"Thanks, Betty," I said, stopping by her car to let her know all was well. She promised to call the next day with the confirmed funeral arrangements and pulled onto SR17, heading north toward Jacksonville.

I tossed the red folder on the passenger seat, tucked my backpack and jacket on the floor, and was just about to exit the parking spot when the rental agent waved me down. I lowered the passenger door window so I could hear him.

"Here's your insurance waiver. I dropped it out of the packet, I'm sorry," he said, leaning in the car to hand it to me. He looked down and a frown formed on his face. I glanced over to see the photo of Richard Jr. peeking out of the folder.

"Did that guy refer you to us?" he asked.

"Do you know this man?" I asked, suddenly unable to breathe.

"Not really, but he rented a car here last week."

## CHAPTER TWELVE

"Said he went to college with my father. He's dead now, though," the car rental attendant continued.

"I see," I muttered, hoping he was referring to his father being dead and not Richard. *No wonder Betty couldn't reach her brother.*

"Are you sure it was this man?"

"I'm sure, ma'am. His mother died in the old mill the same week he was here. Renkin. I thought that was really sad."

"Was he still here when she was found?"

"I don't know. He was going to return the car in Gainesville. Could check with them for you, though. I hope he got to say goodbye to her. Life's hard when people die all of a sudden like that."

Boy, didn't I know *that* fact up close and personal. "Yes, I agree." I swallowed. "Can you find out when that car was returned to Gainesville?"

"Sure, I don't see why not. Want me to call you when I find out? I'd do it now, but the computers are giving me trouble."

I rummaged through my hobo-bag and pulled out my business card case. I handed him a card. "May I have your card, too? Might need to speak to you again, or rent another car, you never know. I appreciate all your help today."

He smiled and reached into his shirt pocket and produced a black and white card. "Thanks," he said. "I'll be sure to give you a call soon." He tapped the door lightly with his palm before turning back toward the shop.

I opted to skip my planned trip to the mill and aimed the car straight for home. My father had information on Richard Jr. that was going to put some of the pieces together, I could just feel it in my bones.

\*\*\*

The pickup was in the driveway when I arrived at the house. I hopped from the slate sidewalk to the porch without touching the steps and almost ran into my father when I charged through the kitchen door.

"Any bites on your homeless guy?" Travis asked.

"Sort of." I snagged a bunch of grapes out of the bowl on the counter and popped two in my mouth. Then I gave him the abridged version of what little we'd learned about the man called "Sarge."

"Nobody knows where he goes off to, right?" he asked.

"That's the story. The Baptist Church on the highway mentioned he may be with the group that camps out by the railroad crossing near the mill." I pulled my sweatshirt up over my head and tossed it into the laundry basket in the pantry. "Where's Papa?"

"Wants to meet us in your office. He's pretty excited."

The fatigue in his voice caught my attention. "Are you feeling okay? You had a long day for someone with a concussion. Everything okay with Margie?"

"I've got a major headache. But Margie's doing fine. I want you to go speak with her, though. There's something she isn't telling me; I can feel it. Maybe talking with another woman will get her to open up."

"You think it's related to the killing itself or the trial? Maybe she's just nervous now that she's finally getting to either trial or release."

He shrugged. "Could be, I guess. And I could be wrong. It's just a hunch, but something's bothering her and like I said, I don't want any surprises if I can help it. I'll only get one shot at a plea bargain, so if she's holding something back, I need to know what it is before we go in tomorrow."

"Okay. I'll go see her tomorrow after church if that's soon enough."

"That'd be fine. Now, let's go catch up with your father, before he paces a hole in the carpeting in there."

My father was at my desk working at the computer. Both printers were working noisily in draft mode, my father's deft grasp catching the sheets before they flew across the room.

"Wow," I said, grinning at him. He looked at me, eyes sparkling with what could only be called glee.

Travis and I sat on the overstuffed sofa, side by side. He pulled my hand into his and we waited for my dad to begin.

"Let's start with Junior, shall we?" he said with gusto.

Using some of the printouts he'd downloaded on my computer, Papa sketched us a verbal picture of the trouble Richard Jr. was facing.

"Federal Trade Commission has indicted him on fraud and several other counts of financial impropriety. His legal fees alone threaten to wipe him out."

"Makes sense why he wanted Matilda to come west, I guess." Travis said. "Someone to help with the kids, someone to help with the money."

"I don't know," I said, "Betty seems to think her mother probably would have helped him regardless. She was desperate to be loved by her son, something he did not demonstrate before now. She was almost ready to move out there, you know. Nobody seems to know what changed her mind. But Betty knew that her brother was having some kind of financial trouble."

Papa continued, not to be deterred by our sidebar discussion. "Richard was the CFO for an umbrella corporation which sheltered a group of smaller corporations. The boards were cross-populated, meaning they shared some members with one another. In most circles this is considered a conflict, but not in all cases. And, had Enron not single-handedly exposed the poor accounting practices of half the corporations in the world, Richard's arrangement would not be suspect even now."

Papa began straightening small stacks of paper and stuffing them into carefully labeled file folders.

"Can he explain the situation away?" I asked. "I mean, did he actually do anything unethical or was he just following the standard business practice for the time?"

"When you tie up your employees' retirement accounts with company stock and then the stock crashes just days after you and your cronies get most of your money safely away, it smells very fishy to the SEC."

"Did all the employees lose everything?"

"Looks that way to me, but remember, finance is my hobby, not my specialty. The fact that he has been indicted means the SEC is very upset with him," my father said sarcastically.

"That's serious enough," he continued. "Of course, in America, we are innocent until proven guilty. But none of that comes without a good deal of stress and character assassination, however."

The afternoon sun filtered in through the wooden window blinds and we sat quietly watching the dust motes dance in the beams of light. I got up and went to the desk, straightening folders that were already perfectly aligned with one another.

"Maybe he came here for money and she refused. Could he have killed his own mother?" I mused.

"There are four basic reasons people kill other people," Travis said. "Passion, fear, greed, and revenge. Most often it's a combination of those emotions. However, until we get those tox results, we don't even know for sure that Matilda was murdered."

"It looks that way, though, Travis. Her car was at her home, so how did she get to the mill? None of the taxi cabs from St. Augustine or Palatka came out here, she didn't walk all that way, and none of her friends dropped her off. That means someone collected her and delivered her there. If this isn't a homicide, how come no one's admitted taking her to the mill?"

"Valid question, but it still doesn't mean she was murdered."

"Let's just pretend we know, okay? Humor me for Pete's sake." I exhaled, ready to find a killer.

My father looked at me. "Matilda was Betty's best ally from what you've told us. What would her motive be for harming her mother?"

"Well, good question. But thank goodness, since she and her husband Michael have an airtight alibi, it doesn't matter. But I have to wonder how Matilda could allow her daughter to suffer like she did, at the hands of old man Renkin. He sounds absolutely diabolical. Hell, I'd like to kill him." I took a deep breath to calm myself. "How much mental and emotional pain can a person endure before they're mad enough to get even?"

"Hmm," Travis sighed. "I don't know. And then what makes one person snap and one person prevail? Lots of people with alibis are still guilty. I hope like hell that Betty's not involved."

"Amen to that. Maybe she didn't kill Matilda, but what about her father? Let me hypothesize for a moment," I said. "She's almost done with nursing school. She's never been able to please the old man, so she decides she's had enough. Or maybe she's doing it to free her mother. Mom's not around, maybe out with Uncle Nate right? Betty argues with good old dad, knowing the stress will drive up the sugar imbalance. She's been home almost two weeks— she knows when he needs his insulin. Maybe she replaced his insulin with water or saline or whatever—he injects himself with useless medication. When he lies down, he never wakes up. She leaves him alone—knows he's going to die and she's glad for it. She's finally free of the bastard."

"Only thing wrong with that idea is that most children will work their whole lives trying to please their fathers, even if they never do," Travis pointed out. "Especially girls. Unless they're psychotic, that is. Then that disapproval might force a split and the other personality would be willing to kill the person inflicting that pain. I don't know Betty, but she doesn't seem psychotic to me."

I stood and placed my pile of printouts on the desk. "I guess that's true, but there are always exceptions. Who suspected Hannibal Lector of his activities? Of course, Richard Jr. was home, too."

"Did Betty tell you that?" Travis asked.

"She mentioned that she thought he was. She isn't real clear about that day." I looked up at him. "Wasn't he there?"

"Not according to the interviews in the file. He's the one who found his father dead in the bedroom. He'd been out with friends all afternoon, came home, and found the old man dead."

"Was Betty home when Junior arrived there?"

"Not if you believe the police reports. She wasn't there at *all* according to her mother. She'd left a note about being out with friends, too. Since foul play wasn't suspected, no one tested the bottles of insulin in the refrigerator, and only a few of the friends were interviewed. Even so, both of their stories held up."

"I guess there's not much hope of reconstructing all of that. Diabetics die all the time." I shuffled through the file and looked over the room inventory from the night old man Renkin died. "They listed a syringe wrapper. No syringe, though."

"Someone might have forgotten to include it, that's all. They weren't looking for anything sinister, remember. Death due to natural causes." Travis rubbed his hands together and looked me in the eye. "You aren't buying this, are you?"

I sighed. "I'm not sure what I believe right now. Or who."

\*\*\*

Sunday afternoon I arranged to visit Margie at the Putnam County Jail. After I was searched and the magazines and novels I brought with me were cleared, I sat in a bare, pale green room waiting for her to join me. I had a cup of coffee that wasn't half bad and sat back to listen to the sounds around me.

The metal clank and bang of the jail doors was a little unsettling. I'd heard it many times before, but I flinched each time one opened and closed. When the door to the interview room swung in, I got to my feet.

Margie was colorless but looked rested at least. I gave her a hug, then we settled at the table. The correctional officer closed the door quietly and I could see her cap through the reinforced window in the door.

"Do you have something to wear for court, tomorrow? Need me to bring you anything?"

"Momma left my Sunday suit and some hair stuff before she left for Alabama. The matron said she was having it pressed for me, so I should be okay, but thanks."

"How are the kids and your mom doing?" I asked, pushing the books and magazines toward her.

She took the reading materials and smiled. "Thank you for these. I sure do love to read. And it helps to pass the time. I'm taking a computer class, too." She smiled and nodded her head. "My family is doing fine. Momma says the baby cries for me once in a while, but they just keep telling her I'll be home soon." She reached into her shirt pocket. "She sent me pictures last week. The baby's walking some."

I took the photos. Taken in front of a small brick church with a tall white steeple, they were dressed in their Sunday best and smiling at the person taking the picture. Life should be simpler when you are nine, seven and two.

"They look great. Your little girl has your hair. She's very pretty. And look how your little one is standing so tall. They're beautiful."

"I hope I can get home soon and send you a family portrait," she said with a tired smile.

"I'm sure you will, Margie. You'll see the judge first thing Tuesday morning and things will move along now. Travis is pushing for either a deal or a speedy trial so you can get back to your children."

"I know. I don't know what I'd have done without his help, Antonia." She looked down at her hands, nails cracked and chipped and in need of polish.

"Have you told Travis everything about the night you killed Brian? I want you to think very carefully before you answer me. Is there *anything* at all you've overlooked? It could be something very small, but important."

She looked at me and sort of stared right through me. I sipped my coffee and waited. Then she shook her head.

"I'm sure I told it just the way I remember it. Travis asked the same thing yesterday. Is there something wrong? You guys sorry you took my case?"

"Oh no, nothing like that. And there's nothing wrong. But he's trying to anticipate what the State's Attorney and the judge may ask, that's all. If he can get you a deal for involuntary manslaughter, he's going to go that way. The State's given him the impression that they're agreeable. This way, the children won't be called as witnesses and the trial wouldn't occur in the papers. Be far easier for them."

"What does 'a deal' mean? I killed him, no sense in denying the truth, Antonia. I was protecting me and my kids."

"You'll have to tell the judge what happened, in your own words. He either believes it was self-defense, which is not punishable by the law, or he decides it was involuntary manslaughter which carries a sentence of less than three years, which means you could be out on parole with time already served. But no trial. Just keep in mind, you're entitled to a trial if you want to go that way. But then there's no deal. At a trial, the outcome depends on what the jury decides."

"I shot Brian in self-defense. He was coming at me with that look on his face. I knew he was going to beat me senseless. The baby was crying. Hell, he'd been crying all day. I was crying all day. Just the idea that Brian would be walking back through that door again was enough to make me sick to my stomach."

I jotted some notes and waited. "Where was the gun, Margie?"

"The one I killed him with? I already told you this. He kept that one in the drawer in the bedroom. As usual, he came through the door looking for a fight. I put dinner on the table, but he wasn't happy with it." She swallowed hard.

"He got up and walked around the table, grabbed me by the hair and forced me to the floor. Then he kicked me in my ribs yellin' about feeding him slop. I started to cry, and the kids were screaming and he yelled at them to go to their room. They ran down the hallway and slammed the door, just like I taught them.

"He dragged me all the way into our room by my hair. I could hear it tearing out of my head and it hurt so bad, worse than my ribs did. He told me to get on the bed and he took off his belt. I curled up in a ball by the pillows, but he went into the bathroom. I ran to the drawer and got the gun. I only wanted him to leave me alone, I just wanted to scare him."

Tears flowed freely down her face, aging her like a watercolor in the rain. I didn't want to stop her recitation, but her pain was palpable. "It's okay, Margie. Take your time."

She wiped her eyes with the back of her hand and squared her shoulders. "He came out of the bathroom and stared at me. Then he started to laugh. Said after he beat me unconscious, he was going to shoot me and feed me to the gators."

"What made you pull the trigger?"

Her head down, she stayed silent. I resisted the urge to pick apart my empty coffee cup while I waited. The clock ticked on the wall, other conversational murmurs drifted through the walls.

When she lifted her face, the tears had stopped. Her hands no longer shook.

"I believed him."

I still hadn't found out what Travis needed to know, but now I knew why he asked me to visit her.

"Margie, you waited almost an hour before calling 911. Why?"

She looked at me with red-rimmed, vacant eyes. The clock on the wall ticked, ticked, ticked for what seemed like forever. Then she smiled, looking like an angel.

"It took me that long to stop laughing."

I shut off the recorder and put my hands on the table. "You may not want to tell that to the judge."

## CHAPTER THIRTEEN

I shuddered and rubbed the goose bumps on my arm. Maybe Travis should have pursued an insanity plea instead. Why hadn't I seen it before? I talked with Margie for hours during the past three months that Travis had been her attorney.

But who was I to judge? I've been angry enough to commit murder a couple of times in my life, though I hadn't followed through. But then, I didn't have kids to protect, so who knows?

I gave Travis the interview tape when I arrived home and we discussed it for a bit. I told him about what wasn't on the tape.

"If she tells him the truth, which of course she should, the plea is out the window," he said, rubbing his fingertips across the bandages on his forehead.

"I know. But at least you have your answer. Relief can make you hysterical, too. The man would never, ever hurt her or scare her kids again. Maybe he'll understand that. Doesn't prove premeditation," I suggested.

"And maybe I'll get lucky enough that he won't ask that one question. I just don't think she cooked this up ahead of time, AJ. She had no way to get herself and the kids away from him. She'd tried it and failed. You can taste her terror when you talk to her."

"I agree. So, you're going ahead with the motion?" I asked, talking over my shoulder as I dragged my tired bones up the stairs to go to bed.

"I am. I still think the self-defense argument will hold up. At worst case, the State's Attorney will tell me no and we go to trial. She'll win hands down, but it will be damned messy for her and the kids."

\*\*\*

"Who was on the phone?" I asked Monday morning as I climbed out of the shower.

"Judge's clerk. He can't see us until later Tuesday afternoon, which works out good for me." He took the towel from my hand and dried my back with firm, but gentle strokes. "Margie wasn't happy about the delay, but overall she's pretty calm. I'm glad it was delayed by hours instead of days or weeks, though."

"She's got to be out of patience with the entire process by now. If she'd had the bail money, she'd be home with her kids, not waiting for a judge to see her."

"And we both know, if she'd been out bail, she and her kids would be sitting targets for the avenging kinfolk."

I conceded his point and went into my dressing room to get ready for the funeral. When I came out, I sat at the antique dressing table he had refinished for me, to put on mascara and gel my hair.

"So, what do you expect at the service today?" Travis asked as he fussed with his "funeral" tie as he called it. It was the only conservative one in his wardrobe. His "courtroom" ties always bordered on contempt of court, but he wore them with style. Funerals unfortunately, didn't lend themselves to music notes and dogs with fishing poles.

I sprayed a few wayward hairs with the White Rain. "I have no clue. Betty was so fragile when she asked us to attend that I didn't push her for any details. Mike's going to be here, some of Matilda's friends, but she never reached Richard, I don't think."

Travis came up behind me and smoothed the shoulders of my brown tweed jacket. "I just talked to the US Marshal's office in Arizona. According to them, the SEC has frozen everything but the wife's accounts. Junior now has less than two thousand dollars available to him."

I smoothed my blouse. "Ouch. Are we working on the assumption that Junior may pose a flight risk? I guess that means he won't be coming out here, then."

Travis shrugged before he answered. "Agent Bodine is just being cautious. Junior's not likely to take off with his kids so entrenched in the community. And they are watching him pretty closely."

"Aha. I know that tone of voice. You plan to be cautious too, don't you? Which means you are not going to give me any peace until we know if he's the killer or not."

He winked and offered his hand. "That's right. I'll try to make protecting you as pleasant as I can."

"Right," I grumbled. "You know, Betty may be in more danger than I am. After all, Richard will have to share the estate with her." *Was he willing to do that, given their cruel childhood relationship?*

"You could be right, especially if Richard killed Matilda, but until we know, I'm keeping a close eye on you. No wandering around by yourself, please."

While we didn't need an argument before appearing before God and all as a happily married couple, I could feel my Arcadian blood pressure rising. "You are not putting me under house arrest over this. I can take care of myself, remember?"

"So can I, but I've got more stitches in my head and face than a raggedy Ann doll. We've both got to be on our best game, right? You need to work with me on this."

116

I grabbed my black gun purse, slipped my wallet and lipstick in it, and walked ahead of Travis to the stairs.

"We'll work it out, okay? We can talk later."

\*\*\*

We parked beside the Presbyterian Church on Main Street and met Betty and Michael in the foyer. With both Betty and I having been gone from Chastity Creek for years, I'd never met him before. She almost crushed me in a hug before introducing us. Michael exchanged greetings with us, then went ahead to his seat.

"He seems like a decent guy, Betty. How you holding up?" I whispered.

She raised one finely-shaped brow. "I've been angry as hell and sadder than I can ever remember. I don't think I have another tear left in my body. Now I'm a little frightened. I'm just worn out, I think."

"Doesn't look like you've gotten much sleep."

Her smile was forced. "Every minute is a struggle. Michael isn't talking much. He's not angry, just sort of brooding. I still can't bring myself to go through my mother's things and I really just want to go home and stay there. I have no desire to be here when my brother arrives next week. He finally called me back."

"We'll talk at the house, okay? I can help you organize the house tomorrow. Lucille will come with me to look at the antiques if you'd like."

117

She nodded and we moved toward the front of the church. "I'd appreciate it. I can't sell anything until my brother gives the okay, but at least I can get things ready and find out more about local prices. Thanks for coming, Antonia."

She looked over my shoulder and nodded. "Travis," she started. Her heel caught on the carpet sending her headlong toward him. He caught her in his arms, holding her until she was steadier. He smoothed her hair back from her face.

"You're going to be okay, Betty. Doesn't feel like it will ever be over right now, but life will resume soon. Just remember that."

She pulled out of his grasp. Without another word, she moved to the front pew and settled next to Michael. Pastor Shelton entered, zipping his purple robe as he walked up the center aisle.

I looked around the sanctuary, noting the small buzz. Perhaps forty people were seated now, five minutes before the memorial service was to begin. Several women, probably in their late seventies or early eighties occupied the last pew, but I didn't recognize any of them. Across the aisle from us, a woman in a gray tailored suit and black veil faced me, but I couldn't see her face in the dim light.

A lovely hand-painted urn stood alone on a white silk cloth at the front of the room. It was not antique, but it was tasteful. Travis and I sat elbow to elbow, each listening to hear whatever we could overhear.

"...poor thing. I wonder if we'll ever know why she was at the factory..."

"Thank God Nathan died first..." I almost turned around at that one, but Travis held me still. *Which one of Matilda's two friends let that one slip?*

"Poor Betty. Now to have trouble with that husband of hers, too..."

"Deserves what she gets, that one. Always thought..."

"Where's her brother? After all Matilda did for that boy, he could at least..."

"Is that Dora?"

The organ started to play *Amazing Grace* and drowned out all the conversations.

*Where was Dora?*

The good pastor was new to the church, but he'd met Matilda when he'd arrived two months ago. He knew how hard she worked around the community. She cleaned the church and she cooked for the shut-ins. He acknowledged that a loving God now had care of Matilda's precious soul and that Betty and Richard could find peace in knowing their mother had been a good woman and was now in the gentle care of a benevolent Father.

Tears ran down Betty's face. Michael reached up several times to wipe them away with his fingertips. She didn't seem to notice.

After the second reading and the third prayer, Pastor Shelton asked if anyone wanted to say a few words. No one stirred. Betty turned around and looked at me.

*Oh no. Me?*

Travis squeezed my hand and then released it. "It's your karma, AJ. Make things right."

Betty stood up and clasped her hands before her. Since they'd chosen not to use the podium, there was no place she could hide them, so there she stood, white-knuckled and stunned.

"My mother had her faults," she began softly, "but she had a kind heart and was stronger than almost anyone I've ever met. I know I left town as soon as I could and stayed away, but she loved me, and I will miss her more than you could possibly know."

I nodded when she stood quiet, hoping she'd know she'd done just fine. She sat down, shoulders stiff and straight. I took the necessary steps forward and took her place.

"Matilda Renkin bore a heavy position in this community. Born from the lineage of a founding family, married to an ambitious man at an early age, she played her role as town matriarch as well as she knew how. It is my impression, that her children meant everything to her.

I respected her tremendously. I sincerely hope that she has found peace at last."

The organ began to play again before I could resume my place beside Travis. He patted my thigh. We all stood as Betty and the pastor walked the red-carpeted isle toward the front porch of the church. Michael followed them. We filed out, row by row, in somber procession.

Several of the church women gathered at the foot of the steps. From the snippets of conversation I could hear, they were helping with the luncheon at Betty's. Mrs. Bradley put a frail hand on my arm and stopped me.

"Will you be going to the house, AJ?"

"Yes, ma'am, I will. Can I take anything over for you? Or do you need me to pick something up?"

"No, dear, we just don't plan on staying very long and wanted to make sure someone would be there. You know, someone her age."

"And someone who's been through this, too?"

She looked away. She was among the group of "Christian" women who'd had no use for my mother, a Catholic Cajun not welcome in this southern Baptist town. My mother'd never seemed overtly bothered by it, but I had always seethed when they snubbed her.

I bit back a remark in honor of that Cajun woman who'd slap me silly, even from her grave, if I was rude. "We'll be there a while. Thank you for your concern."

I turned and took Travis's arm. In a rare, conciliatory move, he patted my hand. His expression said he'd have rather shot the old woman for me.

I gave him a smile, and our small line of vehicles lined up to make our way to the cemetery.

***

Our small procession marched Matilda's ashes into the bright mausoleum. Tiny bronze vases held fresh and silk flowers, all around the room. A newly chiseled marble stone rested on the floor below the vault that would be Matilda's final resting place.

"Goodbye, Mama," Betty said softly as Michael placed the urn up into the niche. Pastor Shelton had us join hands and recite the Lord's Prayer as the sunlight streamed through the stained-glass window at the top of the mausoleum leaving the reflection of a white dove on the floor.

The groundskeeper placed the marble face in place, and we turned to leave. Betty all but collapsed.

"I should have been there, Michael. She shouldn't have died alone."

He wrapped his arms around her, obviously as exhausted as she was. He half-carried, half-escorted her to the limo where the pastor waited. When Betty was seated in the car, he turned to Travis.

"Meet us at the house, would you? My car is at the church, so we have to go back there." He fished around in his jacket pocket and came out with a house key which he handed over. "We won't be long."

Travis and I arrived at the Renkin family home ahead of everyone including the lunch committee and sat outside in the car. I wished Betty had let us just take them to the Cafe for something to eat. Meeting at the house was traditional, but morose as hell. Maybe we would cheer it up with some happy memories, but somehow, I doubted it.

"What's bothering you, AJ?"

"The needles. If you look at the two cases, there are *two* missing hypodermic needles. Where the hell are they?"

"Needles aren't like guns. They aren't traceable, could be thrown anywhere, by anyone. We probably won't ever find out for sure."

I hate it when he's right.

We walked slowly to the house, put the key in the door and stood in the foyer, listening to the silence. Travis left the front door open and hung our coats on the large brass hooks nearby.

I walked into the kitchen and plugged in the big coffee urn that Betty had prepared before she left. Paper plates, cups, napkins, and plastic cutlery were neatly stacked close by. I leaned against the counter and crossed my arms.

"Okay. Regardless of what happened to Richard Senior, who killed Matilda?" I looked at my feet and then at him again. "We know Betty and Mike weren't here when she died.

"If we were clearer on the motive, we'd have a way to work back to the killer. There is little motive to kill Matilda except to gain control to liquidate her assets. Although they gossip like crazy, I can't see the ladies of the church wanting her dead. So, the only ones who gain by doing that are her children." I sighed. My brain was scrambling around in circles.

Travis stared at the floor. "Michael's business is doing well. His cash flow hasn't been great, but he's not ruined, not in catastrophic debt. If he's into organized crime or something, that's another story, but I'm not getting that indication from my sources."

"Yeah, well we both know that greed often has no justification, don't we?"

"Yes indeed. Could be revenge, though. Richard has the larger motive, I guess you could say, but we can't prove he had means or opportunity."

"He *was* here that weekend," I was quick to remind him.

"In the area, not necessarily in town. However, I trust your hunch. He's a strong possibility."

"We still need to know when the car was returned to the rental agency," I said. "That would help."

At that moment, the food brigade arrived straight from the Half-Pot Cafe, so we tabled our conversation. I opted to stay in the kitchen–the same kitchen where I'd listened eleven days ago to Matilda Renkin and her plans to preserve Old Florida history.

Betty and Michael were greeting their small group of guests. Travis had *that* eavesdropping post covered. Matilda's friends found their way into the kitchen.

"Antonia, bless your heart, how nice to see you."

"And you, Mrs. Allison. How are the grandchildren doing?"

"Fine, fine. They all live in Florida now, you know. My daughter Ellen's son—"

"Margaret," interrupted Mrs. Crupnick who owned the bakery, "stop socializing and help me get these pastries into the dining room."

Mrs. Allison looked at me and grinned. I smiled back and watched the two old friends chase each other around, clucking away as they made sure everything was perfectly staged. As Matilda's closest friends, I suppose they thought it was the least they could do.

Three women, I'd guess in their late sixties, joined me, presumably looking for a glass of water. Snooping was more like it. I put ice in a tall clear plastic cup and filled it with water from the pitcher.

"Did you know Matilda, Miss?" one of them asked me. She must have come for the food because she obviously hadn't been in the church for the eulogy.

"Yes ma'am, I've known Matilda and Betty for many years."

"I hear she was a stern woman," the blue-haired woman threw in.

I shrugged. "She was proud, intelligent, and good hearted, but she didn't tolerate a fool, that's for sure."

"Well, she certainly married a fool," the eldest of the trio contributed.

"I didn't know Mr. Renkin very well," I said. "I got the impression he was the stern one."

"A righteous man, for sure," Bluehair announced.

I didn't share my opinion on the topic of righteous people and how they were usually self-righteous instead. I hoped like hell they'd find somewhere else to hang around.

Travis appeared in the doorway and with one raised brow inquired how I was doing. I winked and he disappeared.

My three companions left the kitchen in the awkward silence, and I was glad to see them go. I hoped they'd be considerate of Betty's feelings. Provided of course, they even knew who Betty was. Amazing how many people show up just for the food and gossip at a wake.

Mrs. Allison returned to the kitchen and motioned for me to sit at the table. She poured us coffee and we sighed in unison.

"She's so upset, Betty is. Is there anything I can do to help her?" she asked me.

"I don't know. I think she'll probably feel better when she knows for sure what happened to her mother."

Mrs. Allison paled. "Of course. Then there's this business with the fire at your house. Was that related to Matilda's death?"

I fiddled with my cup. "I have no idea, but the Sheriff's office is looking into it. It was arson, that's all we know for sure."

"It is so upsetting, all these poor manners. What has gotten into people?" she mused as she stirred another spoon of sugar into her coffee.

*Poor manners? Killing people and burning their stuff was poor manners?* I almost laughed out loud, but, of course, *that* would be the *epitome* of poor manners.

"The world has certainly gone crazy, Mrs. Allison. If you see Betty over here, maybe you could stop in and say hello or something. That might make her feel less like a stranger."

"Yoo-hoo, Margaret," called Mrs. Crupnick from the dining room. "Is that coffee ready yet?"

Mrs. Allison sighed again. "What will happen to Mattie's things?"

"Betty's planning to sell almost everything. Of course, that may change when Richard gets here."

She poured coffee from the party urn into thermal carafes. "Did you meet Dora at the church? She's aged twenty years since I saw her last. Nate's funeral, it was."

I picked up a third carafe and moved to her side. "No, I didn't know she was there. Where was she sitting?"

"Right across the aisle from you, dear. She just seemed to vanish though. Did she go to the cemetery?"

"If you're talking about the lady in the black veil, she wasn't at the cemetery." I leaned a little closer so I could speak softly. "Did she visit Matilda, much? Betty seemed to think maybe there was bad blood between them."

"Mattie was always nervous as a long-tailed cat in a room full of rockers when Dora was around. And to be honest, Dora's a touch strange, at least around Betty. Now Nate, he adored that child and made sure she had all she needed, but then I think he was sweet on Mattie, too. And I think Dora always thought Senior was *her* man anyways.

"After Mattie and Dora's mama died in '42, their daddy, Joshua Mayfield, sent Dora to a finishing school, you know. Wanted her to be a professional. Their father arranged their lives for them. Back then, that's how life was, not like today with every child doing whatever they please, with no regard for anyone else."

She screwed on the lid to the carafe and wiped the sides clean. "Mattie had no intention of marrying, but without sons, her father wanted someone smart to take over the business."

"Too bad he didn't know Matilda was smart enough in her own right."

"It simply wasn't done, my dear. Even though Dora was the eldest daughter, when old man Mayfield was ready to step down, he wanted a good businessman to take the reins and he wanted Matilda to be taken care of. Personally, I don't think Richard was a good choice for *anything*."

Margaret was summoned yet again, and we took the coffee into the dining room and set it on the mahogany sideboard. The cut crystal sugar bowl and creamer pitcher stood at attention nearby.

"Let's get something to eat dear, and then we'll get these vultures out of here. Betty needs to get some rest," she whispered in my ear. I agreed, but I wanted to see if I could find Dora.

An hour and a half later, though several people thought they'd seen her at the church, Dora was nowhere to be found.

Betty, Travis, Michael, and I had the food packed up and the house back in order in no time. The only thing left to clean was the party percolator, so I got to it. Betty joined me and sat at the kitchen table.

"Betty, did your Aunt Dora come to the house? I heard she was at the church."

"I thought that was her sitting across from you, but I wasn't all that sure. When we got finished, I went to speak to her, and she was gone. And I didn't see her here. I'm glad I didn't imagine the whole thing."

"Maybe it was just too much for her. Does she have any children?" Curiosity was prickling at me like static during an electrical storm.

Betty shook her head as she dried her hands on an embroidered linen dish towel. "She and Uncle Nathan had a daughter, but I think she died when she was a baby."

"How awful." Lord, this family had more than its share of hard luck, that was for sure.

"I was really little. You know, after I was ten, I don't think I saw her a dozen times. Last time was at Uncle Nate's funeral."

"I guess you don't know if your mother saw her at all?"

She shook her head. "No, I'm sorry. Somehow, I don't think so. She's just always been sort of...forgettable. Isn't that sad?"

I dried the coffee urn and tucked the power cord inside. "It is. But we can't change all that, so please don't dwell on it. Anything else you need before we head out?"

We walked to the front room where Michael and Travis waited for us.

She picked up her jacket and Michael held it for her. "No, everything looks great. Thanks so much for all your help, both of you," she said. Travis bent to kiss her cheek and smiled.

We walked to the door together. Betty and Michael were obviously not staying in the family home tonight. Michael turned to Travis.

"We'll be at the Best Western if you need us for anything." They shook hands. Betty locked the front door while I waited.

"What time do you want me here tomorrow?" I asked.

"Is eight too early? Richard called last night. He told me to just box up Mother's things. I'm to take what I want and donate or sell the rest. He said he didn't care about any of the antiques."

"How was he?"

"He sounded very tired. He's in a lot of trouble with the government and he knows it. I don't know if he can even leave the state of Arizona right now. He was friendlier to me than he's ever been, but I didn't ask a lot of questions."

I walked her to the car where Michael was waiting.

"Thanks for your help, AJ," Michael said, offering me his hand.

"Didn't do much, but you're welcome, Michael. I saw you and Travis talking, I'm sorry I didn't get to join you. Are you doing okay?"

He nodded. "I'm worried about Betty, but I'm fine." He reached out to pull Betty into his arms. I smiled and turned toward our car.

Travis opened the car door for me, I got in and we drove to the Café.

It was quiet, so Lon and Kathy sat a few minutes with us.

"How did it go? I was two waitresses short, so I couldn't leave," Kathy apologized.

"It was a simple service, small attendance, but nice group. You did a wonderful job with the food, guys. Matilda would have been proud of how well her guests were taken care of."

"It was the least we could do. I feel so bad for Betty. Wish we could help."

I laughed. "Two weeks ago, you thought she killed her mother."

Kathy looked shocked, then grinned. "But *you* didn't. And when I actually gave it some thought, I decided I'd put my money on you. Now, she may have killed that rat-bastard of a father, but I don't think she killed her mother."

Travis and I looked at each quickly. He spoke softly. "Why do *you* think she killed her father?"

Lon looked over his shoulder. "Gossip, that's why. We hear a lot, but we don't know anything. Most townspeople thought he was a tough businessman, but a great guy."

"Yeah, and Ted Bundy's neighbors thought he was a nominee for Man of the Year," she pointed out, poking him in the ribs with her elbow.

The bell rang over the door and Lon got up to handle the customer. Kathy leaned forward.

"When she was just a little thing, she used to come in here with bruises. Never looked anyone in the eye unless she was with her mother, and I don't think I ever saw her happy. Not really happy if you get my meaning. My guess is the old man was hurting that child."

"You may be right. And it's a damned shame, because I don't know if people ever fully recover from stuff like that."

"And who killed Matilda? Any ideas about that one?" Kathy asked as she stood to leave.

Travis shook his head. "The Sheriff's office is still working on it."

She nodded and straightened her apron. "Gotta go. If we can do anything, let us know."

For another few minutes, we enjoyed the soft chatter around us. As we stood to leave, Travis's cell phone buzzed. He glanced at it, then tucked it back in his jacket pocket.

"You? Not taking a call? What's that about?" I poked him in the chest with my index finger as I put my bag on my shoulder.

"No more calls today. Beside it was a text."

Aha. I wasn't going to ask him who it was. *Nope. I didn't even care who it was.* I pushed through the door into the damp November gray.

"Okay, who was it?"

I heard his chuckle behind me. "You did good, Trouble. Took you almost thirty seconds to cave in." I turned and swatted at him, but he side-stepped me, grinning from ear to ear.

I got in the car and fastened the seatbelt. "You up for a ride?" he asked.

I glanced at him and shrugged. "Sure. Where to?"

"I thought we'd pay our respects to one of the missing characters."

I was clueless, so I waited for an explanation that was apparently not forthcoming. Sometimes it annoyed me that he can play me like a fiddle. I sighed.

"And who would that be?"

He made the turn toward SR20 and switched on the radio. "Someone who could be a bigger player in this game than we thought..."

# CHAPTER FOURTEEN

Dorathea Mesters, it turned out, lived just south of Gainesville, Florida, near the little town of Arredondo. Her neatly tended tin-roofed home was bordered by several acres of fresh-tilled earth. Farming soil so alive I could smell it in the air. Bare-limbed black oaks ringed the fields. Ancient palms sprouted up like green and brown exclamation points.

The yellow clapboard farmhouse was set back off the road about a hundred feet. A tired Golden Retriever struggled to his feet when we parked behind the vintage gold Cadillac Coup de Ville near the barn. A symphony of glass and metal chimes greeted us when we climbed the steps to the covered porch.

The heavy door had an oval stained glass inset of a massive Florida oak tree. I was appreciating all the intricate color and lead beading when it opened. I forced my jaw to stay together. Looking at Dorathea was like looking at Matilda Renkin, years ago.

"Mr. Buchanan, I assume?" she asked without opening the screen door. She had a hand-embroidered black cardigan draped over her shoulders and she leaned on a mahogany cane.

Travis nodded. "This is my wife Antonia, Mrs. Mesters. Thank you for seeing us."

She unlatched the screen and pushed the door wide to let us in. "You stay," she commanded. I stopped.

"Not you, *him*," she said, pointing her cane at the old dog. He ducked his head and stretched out in the pale sunshine at the foot of the steps. "He's a nuisance when I have company. It will do him some good to stay in the fresh air."

I stepped around her and waited at Travis's side. Dora led us into a spacious living room, just off the entryway. "Would you like tea?"

I nodded my head. "That would be nice, thank you, Mrs. Mesters. We wanted to tell you how sorry we are about Matilda. Betty told us you were at the funeral service, but when we didn't see you at the house, we thought we'd check and make sure you were all right."

I watched her as I spoke. No emotional response of any kind. Finally, she smiled at me, but it never reached her gray-blue eyes.

"Betty is mistaken, I didn't attend Matilda's funeral. Only dead people have funerals and Matilda is most certainly not dead. She and I spoke just a few days ago."

She rubbed her hands together and then sat back in the chair, pulling her sweater around her shoulders. "Besides, I'm an embarrassment to her and all the family. None the less, if Matilda was dead, I'd have driven to the service if I wasn't nursing this bad hip. It would be so good to see Betty again. I took a fall a week ago and just can't get around like I should."

I glanced sideways at Travis. "Did you speak with Matilda before, or after, your fall?" I asked. "Do you remember?"

"Of course, I remember. I'm not addle-brained, you know. I spoke to her *after* my fall. She called to tell me she was going to move to Arizona to live near Junior."

"Do you and Junior visit often, Mrs. Mesters?" I asked.

"I told you, I'm not considered part of the family. I don't visit with anyone."

"That must be hard for you, to be all by yourself. Do you have friends who visit you, I hope?"

"I have a great many friends, Mr. Buchanan. Friends from the old days at the Creek, and church friends that come by almost every day. Everyone is always very helpful. The doctor said I should be fine in another few weeks. The injuries could have been worse."

"How'd you do it? Fall down those front porch steps?" I asked.

She looked at me as though she'd forgotten what she'd just related. "Oh, the damned dog. Got up to answer the phone at the same time he got up to eat. We tripped over each other, that's all."

I nodded and looked around the room while Travis made small talk about her home, the unchecked housing expansion in the area, and Betty.

"Let me make that tea for you," Dora said, struggling to get to her feet. Travis jumped up and assisted her, offering to help her with the refreshments. She looked at me.

"I do believe I will take the help from your husband if you don't mind, Mrs. Buchanan."

"Not at all. He enjoys helping whenever he can," I replied with a smile aimed at him.

"Yes, I'm sure he does. Men who offer their help so freely can be quite devious though, did you know that?"

Without waiting for a reply, she turned toward the hallway with a puzzled Travis at her side. I shrugged and he nodded and then followed behind her. I decided to take an unsupervised look around the long room.

I only glanced at the photos quickly. There weren't many, and none of the man I knew as Nathan Mesters but then he'd been dead, what, ten years?

A worn, oak writing desk sat at the farthest end of the parlor, facing the large windows that when opened, would certainly ventilate the entire room. Along the wall closest to the desk were built-in bookcases filled with classic-titled leather-bound books. A barrister's case contained current computer manuals for most of the popular applications.

I walked to the desk and noticed a large laptop, closed and silent. I could hear Travis talking with Dora, so I didn't dare start it up to see what she did with it. Probably wrote up the church bulletins or something benign. I was seeing psyco-poets everywhere these days.

I turned to go back to the sofa at the other end of the room, when I spotted something in the wire mesh trash can beside the desk. I reached in, snagged it, and tucked it into my jacket pocket. *Ah ha.*

I was standing in front of the brick-faced fireplace, looking over the wood-framed photos when they returned.

Travis set the tea tray on the table and poured three cups from the rosewater patterned pot.

"Betty is a very nice young woman," he started, stirring sugar into his tea. "You must be proud of her. She said she went into nursing because you inspired her. She's not ashamed of you at all."

When he mentioned Betty, Dora smiled. "I was a nurse for almost forty years. But the whole business is just too much for an old woman, these days. More and more degrees are needed, AIDS, and other devil-spawned diseases are running rampant and no one really cares about healing any more. I've been working with computers for nearly ten years now. It keeps my mind sharp and my hands useful, you know. Idle hands are the Devil's helpmates, and all that."

I thought Travis was going to spit out his tea. "What type of work do you do, Mrs. Mesters?" I asked.

She shrugged and sipped from her cup. "I teach old people how to use computers, of course. Email and letter writing, just simple things like that. They have to learn, or they cannot stay in touch with their families. No one has time to visit anyone these days, you know."

"That does seem to be true, I'm sad to say," Travis muttered.

There were two family portraits on the mantel. Richard Sr. and Dora were smiling, holding a white-bundled infant. By the cut of their clothes, the picture had to have been taken in the 1960's. The other was a picture of Richard Jr. in his college graduation garb.

When Travis let the conversation lapse, I pointed to the picture. "That's Richard Jr., isn't it?"

She looked over her shoulder and nodded without looking at me. "Yes, it is. We were so proud of him. A son that made Richard proud."

"Have you seen him lately?" I asked.

"I believe I told you, I'm the 'black sheep', Mrs. Buchanan. I don't see any of them."

"The other picture, is that Richard Sr. with Betty, perhaps?"

"That photo was taken the day my daughter was christened. With her Uncle Richard. She died later, you know."

She looked at me with a sadness that was almost tangible. Were the teary eyes for the child, the man, or the memories?

"I can see by your expression that you know I lost that child. You need not pity me. It was a long time ago. We live to serve the Lord. We can't change His will."

"You're right, of course," I said softly. "Still, I am sorry for any mother who loses a child. The circumstances seldom make that an easy thing."

"Most of life is not easy, is it? And sometimes, the Lord takes that child for a very good reason. What do you really want to know, Mrs. Buchanan?"

"Would you know who would want to harm Matilda?"

The twitch in the corner of her left eye was so quick, I might have imagined it. "So, she *is* dead then? And someone thinks it was murder?" She placed her teacup on the tray and got to her feet. "As I said, we weren't close. I would have no idea who would want to harm her. Maybe you should ask Betty's handsome husband." She looked pointedly at Travis.

"I don't understand. Why do you think Michael may have wanted to harm Betty's mother?" he asked.

"She had money, and she certainly wouldn't allow anyone to harm her child. A mother's job is to keep her children safe, is it not? If she doesn't do that, she has no purpose. She should cease to exist. In some counties, the males of the family are charged with that duty, you know. They determine the fates of their female family members."

I put my cup down and clasped my hands in front of me. "In the Middle East that is true, Mrs. Mesters."

"And here in the south, as well. Always, in the aristocratic southern family, men do as they please for the good of the families."

"Do you have any specific reason to believe that Michael is hurting Betty in some way? Or that they need Matilda's money?"

She waved her hand in dismissal. "Men always hurt their women, don't they? And money makes people do very unsavory things. I've seen a lot of that in my years. In nursing, you see a lot. The things done to sick and elderly folks by their own kin would just make you sick to your stomach. It sure did to me."

The silence stretched on and our tea grew cold, untouched in the beautiful porcelain cups. Travis cleared his throat and I nodded at him. He stood and offered me his hand.

"Please don't get up, Mrs. Mesters. We'll see ourselves out and again, our sincere sympathies on the death of your sister. The police are investigating it, so I'm sure they'll keep you informed of their progress."

She studied us, pulling her sweater closer. "They needn't bother, Mr. Buchanan, nor should you. Matilda's death simply closes another chapter in the unseemly Mayfield family history. It doesn't concern me." She stood and then put her hand on my arm. "Betty is safe, right? I mean, you won't let any of this harm her, will you?"

I nodded at her. "Betty will be fine, and we'll watch out for her. You should call her next week. I think she'd enjoy talking with you."

We said goodbye and headed for the car, careful not to trip over the damned dog. Poor thing didn't look like it could get out of its own way, let alone into someone else's, but who knew. Travis didn't say a word until we were back onto SR20 and heading due east.

"Coffee?" he asked. "We can stop at Carla's up the road if you want. She might even have some sweet potato pie which you love so much."

"Sure, then you can explain how Dora knew we were coming. Quite a few surprises for me today. And who the heck is Carla? Care to enlighten me?" I asked.

"I'll introduce you to her. Your lovely hazel eyes will turn green with envy when you meet her."

"Right," I said, wondering what he was up to. "Was that little talk with Dora the oddest conversation you ever had or what? Is she completely nuts?" I stared out the window as we slowed at the light. "I wonder if any of them know anything at all about love? Betty seems to be the only one that has a clue."

He left me alone with my mutterings and we drove for several sparsely populated miles. He turned into the roadside restaurant on the two-lane highway and shut off the engine.

"Oh, it was odd all right." He laughed. "I don't know if she's truly a bit daft or if that's an act. She seemed completely coherent, yet why pretend she wasn't at the funeral? Wish I'd checked out the car a little better. "

"Would have been tough to do that without being conspicuous, parked all the way under the carport. Notice the *only* real reaction we got was when I asked about Betty?"

"Yeah, but she covered it quick. And she's lying about Junior, too. Why did he fly into this airport last week if not to see her?"

"She's either lying or she's got some other mental issue. Maybe Alzheimer's or something?"

He held the restaurant door for me and we seated ourselves in a booth. The waitress, who was all of seventeen, had purple hair and a ring through her nose. She grinned when she saw my earrings.

"Cool loops," she said between chomps on her gum.

"Thanks," I murmured as I took the laminated four-page menu from her.

We ordered coffee and she meandered off.

Travis' phone buzzed again. He pulled it out of his pocket and looked at it, then put it away. Again, he didn't answer it. "So, what's the theory now, Trouble? Does Dora have a role in all this or is she just another dysfunctional member of the Mayfield clan?"

I sipped my coffee and shrugged. "Who's on the phone, Travis? And why are you being so mysterious? If you feel the need to never take your eyes off me until this is solved, we've got a real problem. And how did Dora know we were coming for a visit?"

He fiddled with the cutlery. *Hmmm.* The eighty-five-pound waitress came back with enough creamers to fill a soup bowl. He stared out the window before he looked back at me.

"I asked Summer to do some digging around and give us a hand. You've been pretty busy. Dora doesn't own that property, which is why you couldn't find her through the normal channels."

"How did Summer find it, then?"

"Your DMV information helped. We knew Dora was in Florida somewhere. Or at least someone by that name. Once I knew what Junior's corporate information was, I had Summer do a search of all Florida property owned under that name. Voila."

"Summer's very capable, isn't she?" I asked, wondering half-heartedly if that idea bothered me. "If I go to Washington for a while, at least you'll have a replacement for me all ready to go."

He stirred in another creamer and held onto the spoon. "There will never be a 'replacement' for you, AJ. And about Washington. Is that going to be something we discuss or are you just going to pack up and leave me a note after a night of wild sex and expect me to wait patiently at home."

"Of course, we'll discuss it. But I don't know how I feel about it yet, so much has happened with Matilda, my father, and you. Flynn keeps calling and he's stuck on the idea that maybe if I go back there, we can put the Rick investigation to bed once and for all." I was drawing milky circles on the napkin with my spoon.

"What's your gut telling you?" he asked evenly.

"Well, how the hell are you, Yankee?" bellowed a sixtyish, full-sized woman in jeans and a blue and white checked blouse, sporting bright red hair with a pencil stuck in it. I almost jumped out of my seat.

Travis looked up and smiled. "Carla darling, I'm just fine. Want you to meet my wife, AJ."

Carla shook my hand and I thought I heard the bones in my fingers snapping. "You two are looking mighty serious for lovebirds. Everything okay?"

Travis nodded. "Things will lighten up if we can talk you out of that sweet potato pie of yours."

"Whipped cream, too?" she asked with a grin.

"Absolutely," I chimed in. "Heard it's the best sweet potato pie in the state of Florida. Bet the whipped cream is, too."

146

Carla nudged Travis' shoulder. "She's as smart as you said she is. I'll go get those pie orders for ya'll." She moved with the grace and agility of an experienced waitress.

"So," Travis began, adeptly changing topics, "do you have any new theories on who killed Matilda, or do the old ones still feel right to you?"

I wiped my hands on the large paper napkin. "I don't know what I think at this point. If Dora thought Matilda's daughter was really Nathan's, then jealousy or revenge are great motives for murder."

"Yes, but she isn't in physical condition to overpower her sister. You can't overlook ability. Goes to means and opportunity. And don't forget, the toxicology results aren't back yet. We don't know beyond a shadow of a doubt that she was murdered at all."

"Sure we do, Travis. As far as Dora goes, you're taking her word for her whereabouts and her injury. Maybe it's all baloney. And then, there's Junior. She isn't all that far from the Gainesville airport which is where Junior supposedly returned the rental car. Maybe she's covering for him."

"Yeah, there is that. She clearly lied about her relationship with Junior. The farm is owned by him, so he's had to be in contact with her, probably on a regular basis."

I shrugged. "Maybe I'll get a better handle on it all when I see Betty tomorrow. We're missing a piece. It's a critical piece, too. I've been thinking the killer was Junior, but I certainly could be wrong. How did he get out of Arizona without your marshals knowing, I wonder?" I was tired and eager to get home and look over what I had tucked in my pocket.

"I don't think he was under as much surveillance, then. That happened after I alerted the US Marshals that he'd been here."

"Well, that will endear us to him, won't it?" I thought aloud. "And what was Dora talking about the men in a family have the right to exterminate the women?"

"Got me," Travis said, looking up when the pie was delivered. "I've heard of it in middle eastern cultures, but not here. Off and on I clearly got the idea that she was pretty confused. Could be a form of dementia, I suppose. Not many people we can ask about it, though. Maybe we can track down her church friends or something."

"Now that would stir up the beehive for sure. Maybe we'll just wait on that," I said, forking a piece of pie into my mouth. I almost moaned out loud.

The pie lived up to my husband's description and we devoured it in silence. I fought the urge to lick the plate.

We finished our coffee and Travis tossed money on the table for the waitress's body-piercing fund before we moved to the register. He straightened my collar as he waited for Clara to come ring up our check.

"You didn't answer me about Washington. If you have a plan, I want to hear it, AJ. Rick may have been your husband then, but I'm your husband now. I'm not going to happily let you go traipsing off to investigate a murder, especially one that was set up by the Agency."

"I don't have an answer for you, Travis. I haven't made up my mind. When I do, I'll let you know. For now, let it rest, okay? I don't poke a stick into your ghosts, respect mine."

"My ghosts are handled, yours aren't. Don't forget to include me, that's all I'm asking. I love you. Just remember I'm on your side, honey."

He paid the bill and we got back in the car. On the road again, I relaxed and looked out the window.

"Richard's coming out next week, you know," I said.

We'd gone five miles before Travis spoke again. "I don't want you meeting him unless I'm with you, okay? If he contacts you, the correct answer is you will get back to him."

*I don't think so* that little voice in my head taunted. "I have work to do, Travis. I don't intend to stay cooped up until you have the time to let me out, like a puppy on a leash."

"If I have to hire a watchdog, AJ, I'll do it. Don't forget, you've received death threats and they were directly related to this case. I almost burned to death a few days ago and we don't know it wasn't related. We aren't going to ignore the possibilities."

"I'm not ignoring them. And I'm not proposing to be careless, but I'm not going to be a prisoner in my own home either."

"We could take some time off and get lost for a few weeks. How about the islands? Or that Ireland trip we always talk about taking?"

Now it was my turn to laugh out loud. "In your dreams, Travis. I told you before; I'm not running from this. Southern women don't run away, they fight back."

"This isn't about you being a southern woman, it's about you being too damned stubborn for your own good. I don't know what I'll do if anything happens to you."

I looked at him and grinned like a five-year-old. "Same back at cha," I drawled.

## CHAPTER FIFTEEN

I bounded down the stairs on Tuesday morning, ready for hot coffee, prepared by our own personal assistant, forever to be known as Asta. My father had cajoled me out of setting the automatic timer and allowing the system to handle it.

Although the fire marshal had ruled the explosion at Dad's place an accident, repairs to his house were taking forever and I felt it important to humor him. Our security system proved a worthy distraction from his impatience.

Pulling a Jacksonville Jaguar mug from the cabinet, I reached for the coffee. Although it was brewed, it was quite cold. I poured a cup anyway and stuck it in the microwave to heat it up. The timer was flashing on the coffee maker. Evidently Asta's backup system wasn't all it should have been, and the mighty assistant had been felled by a little power outage. We had quite of few of those, unexplained to date by the great power company.

I emptied the carafe and manually started a fresh pot for Travis. He had a full court calendar, including finishing the work for the plea hearing on Margie's case. Judge Fishburne had a reputation as a tough but fair judge. The State Attorney's office was not up for reelection this year, so Travis was optimistic that he could get Margie freed as soon as the end of this week, if the judge would approve the sentencing recommendations as well.

I was in the process of stirring grits into the pot of melted butter and milk when the phone rang.

"Hello?" I asked, peering at the caller ID. I listened, removing the milk from the hot burner before I had a catastrophe.

"I see. Well, thanks for letting me know and go get some sleep. You have to be totally beat." I replaced the phone receiver back on the hook.

"Who was that, honey?" Travis asked, his tie and top shirt button still undone as he sat down at the kitchen table.

"Shane Davis. The tox reports on Matilda are back. No drugs, but her blood glucose number was over seven-hundred. There's no diabetes history for her with any of her doctors."

"Needle sites?" he asked, stirring sugar into his coffee.

152

"One possibly up near the hair line on the back of her neck. A little hard to be sure with decomp starting when she was found."

"Looks like your gut was correct all along, AJ. Have they called Betty yet?"

"Just before he called me. She asked him to explain it to me himself. Said she'd see me later at Matilda's house."

"You two need to be very, very careful, do you hear me? Lock yourselves into the house if you have to. And keep your eyes open for anyone who shouldn't be there."

"Will do. Beside me and Betty, Kathy's coming by with her grandson for a little while, and I've invited Lucille to come and appraise the antiquities. Everyone else will be shot on sight."

He laughed and grabbed my waist as I dashed by the table. "Don't shoot anyone, okay? I'm pretty busy right now. At this rate, I'll have to hire an attorney just to handle my family affairs."

"Wise ass," I mumbled while I freed myself. Those poor grits were doomed. I reached the stove a second before they boiled over.

"What time are we due in chambers this afternoon?" I asked, spooning breakfast into the bowl.

"Three-thirty. Did the paper get here this morning?"

"It's here," Papa said, carrying it under his arm. "Much less news here than in Gainesville," he said.

Turning to me, he smiled. "How was your coffee this morning?"

I laughed. "Tasty, but cold, Papa. We must have had a power outage last night. Happens a lot here."

He frowned. "There must be something wrong with the battery backup system. I will have to see about that." He sat down across from Travis. "Your attorney friend called me yesterday while you were out. We will speak today to the insurance company. They do not want to pay any more for the repairs."

Travis put down his fork and steepled his long fingers. "Would you like me to be on the call? I'm not due into court until this afternoon."

Papa shook his head. "I will tell the truth to him. If you legal minds need to discuss it, you may do so at your leisure. And I will pay him myself, is that understood?"

"Don't worry about it, Henri."

"I am not worried, and I can afford to pay. I appreciate you finding me someone who can be trusted. It will work out as it must."

Coffee lodged in my throat as it warred with my tears. He could lose his job, his pension, and his lovely home. He smiled at me.

"Do not worry, Antonia. Everything will be fine. After all, it isn't as though I meant to blow up the house. I'm a scientist, not a terrorist."

I nodded since I couldn't speak. I gave both of the men in my life a hug, then escaped to a hot shower.

\*\*\*

My jeans were worn out in the knees which I didn't figure mattered much to clean a house that was over a hundred years old. My gray and maroon Georgetown University sweatshirt was paint-stained. And psychologically, I was raring to go. Purse, jacket, and camera bag in hand, I headed for the rental car.

"Lucky Lucy's" baby-blue van pulled up in front of the house at the same time I did. Lucille and I climbed the driveway together. Betty and Michael's yellow Mustang was already parked by the kitchen door. A short roll-off trash container was pulled alongside the porch. Betty wasn't kidding about cleaning up. It was already half full of boxes and jars and several mattresses and box springs.

Someone yelled for us to come in when I knocked, so we did. We made our way into the kitchen. When in doubt, follow the nose. Blueberry muffins was my bet.

"Kathy!" I nearly shouted when we came through the doorway. She had her grandson by the hand as though she knew exactly how much destruction would be caused if she let him go.

"Thought I'd bring Betty some breakfast. Have you eaten yet?"

"Nope," I said, making a beeline for a mug of coffee and a muffin the size of a softball. "I burned the grits. How'd you know we'd be here this morning?"

She grinned at me. "Lucy stopped in. The rest is history in this town."

"Cool. Glad she did," I said, taking a bite. Nothing better in the whole world than homemade muffins. "You going to stay a while?"

She aimed her chin at little Tommy. "That would *not* be wise. Nor good for my mental health. However, his dad is home early today since he worked last night. I'll stop back around lunch time, okay?"

"I'm going to play with my daddy today," Tommy said around a toothless smile. I winked at him.

Betty joined us. "I really appreciate this, Kathy. I'm determined to get this done today." She smiled at Tommy who grinned back. "Just come in. The door won't be locked with us in and out all day."

"I have to meet Travis at the courthouse at three-thirty for the hearing, so I may work through lunch."

Kathy gave me a quick hug and disappeared with offspring gently in tow. Betty and I laughed at the same time. "Let's get at it, then. Where do you want to start?" I asked.

Lucille spoke up, all business as usual. Her bright red hair fit her outgoing personality perfectly. She was bold, but not harsh. A woman with a good reputation in the antique business.

"I'd like to start on the first floor if that's okay. I'll do the bedrooms last."

Betty shrugged. "Okay by me. The only two rooms I don't want to deal with are my mother's bedroom and her office, which are connected." She touched my arm lightly.

"If you'd manage those for me, I'd appreciate it. I'll work the library first. I've promised Mother's collection of classics to the university." She looked at her watch. "They'll be here at ten-thirty. I need to have that ready."

And that, was that. I used my camera to document the rooms in their current state. Then I photographed each piece of furniture, and when I'd laid out the contents of each drawer and the closet on the bed, I photographed that, too. Then I wrote out a brief catalog of the items as I boxed them and sealed the boxes shut.

I was wiping out the inside of the bottom drawer of Matilda's solid walnut bureau when I realized I'd missed something. My pinky hit something wedged way in the corner. I groped around and got my fingers around it. A tiny cardboard envelope. A repaired ring maybe? Some gift from Nathan that had to be hidden?

I knelt on the floor and dropped the dust cloth. I opened the pouch slowly. It contained a tiny key. Locket key? Too small for a suitcase or a clock.

I dropped it in the pocket of my flannel shirt and finished cleaning the drawers, barely able to concentrate.

I bet that Matilda Renkin had a diary.

\*\*\*

A careful search of the desk and shelves in Matilda's office were of no use. Matilda was meticulous, not getting ready to die. She hadn't known what was in store that week any more than the rest of us. I found comfort in that realization. She hadn't died because I missed an important hint of some kind.

I gathered up all of her household files and checkbook, bank, and insurance records and clearly marked the box for Betty. Nothing was past due. Insurance policies for Matilda and both of her children were paid up for another year.

I taped up the box, put Betty's name and the contents on the outside and piled it on the floor by the Queen Anne desk. When Kathy called up the stairs, it was almost one-thirty. My assigned areas were complete.

We met in the kitchen, tired, smudge-faced, and willing to laugh at Kathy's antics. A true Southern girl, our Kathy. Unable to do much else, she kept us well fed.

With the exception of the kitchen set, all the furniture now sported little tags marked Lucky Lucy's on one side and a dollar value on the other.

"You and Richard are going to have a lot to talk about. You're looking at a lot of assets here," I said. Betty made a face.

"Not worth it for a life, is it? If I could sell it all and get my mother back, I would."

"Mothers are best friends when we're this age."

"She was always my best friend." Betty sipped at her coffee and reached behind her to the countertop. She pulled over a leather book the size of ledger. My heart skipped a beat, then began to pound harder. At least until

I saw there was no clasp. It wasn't the book I'd been searching for.

"What's that?" I asked, leaning forward to take a closer look.

"My father's personal ledger. I found it in the library when I was boxing the books. I wonder why my mother kept it."

She'd gone a little pale. Kathy and I exchanged a look that warned us to brace for more bad news but we stayed quiet.

"My father never paid one dime of my college expenses. He paid every cent of Richard's, but not a penny towards mine. My Uncle Nate and my mother paid everything not covered by my scholarship. Daddy really did hate me, didn't he?" she whispered to no one in particular.

"Betty, from what I can tell, your father wasn't exactly a kind-hearted man. I'm sure his behavior had nothing to do with you."

Tears gathered in her eyes, but she banished them with a shake of her head. "I'm not so sure. He was a hateful man who ran around pretending to be a good Christian. He chased my Aunt Dora away. He was brutal to my mother. She deserved so much more happiness."

I reached over and took the book from her hands. "She knew some, Betty. And you made her very happy. She was very proud of you, I know that."

"She was so hurt and angry with me the last time I saw her. I really thought that she wanted to be with my brother, or I would never have tried to help him convince her to go. She always wanted his love and didn't get it. I didn't want to lose her, but I wanted her to be happy. At first, she really sounded like she wanted to go."

She broke down in tears, burying her head in her arms as though sobbing away years of pain and disappointment. Kathy and I busied ourselves cleaning up the kitchen, keeping one eye on our battered hostess. After several minutes, she got up from the table and went into the bathroom off the pantry.

At a little past two o'clock, Kathy and I moved to pack up the linens that were neatly starched and stacked on the lowest pantry shelf. When we had it all boxed and labeled, Betty closed the door after wiping the shelves clean.

Her voice seemed old. "She was able to take care of herself, why didn't she leave my father? Why let him hurt her so much? Why let him hurt *me* so much?"

"I have no idea why she didn't leave. Maybe she thought she couldn't take care of you properly or maybe she was more afraid to leave than to stay."

Her laugh sounded like rusty and forced. "Right. She had her own money, a good name. I don't care anymore, I just don't understand it, that's all."

I stacked the box on the table in the kitchen. "You were in nursing, so I'm sure you saw battered women at some point in your training or internship."

She turned with a dust rag still in her hands. "I saw some, sure. Especially in the Emergency Room, but they were almost bag ladies. Not women like my mother."

I considered what words to use to help her understand. I'd seen too many victims, too often. And all too often, I'd been powerless to help even in a small way. But I learned to understand.

"In Washington D.C., I did one of my first photographic series for the *Post*. I spent weeks in the shelters for battered women. I rode along with the DC cops if a domestic disturbance call came in. Many of them were women very much like your mother, Betty. Educated, intelligent and horribly afraid of starting over alone. Add kids in, it was only worse for them. Some of them were wives of very cruel, powerful men."

"That's a big city, AJ. This is a small town where she was surrounded by people who knew her from the time she was a little girl. Surely, someone would have helped her if she'd asked."

"I don't know the answers, Betty. I'm just saying, try not to judge your mom too harshly. I know without a doubt she loved you. Something made her stay. If we find her diary, you might know more."

She straightened and looked at me. "Diary?"

161

I pulled the tiny keys out of my pocket and held them in my palm. "I think these are keys to a diary. Or maybe more than one."

She stared at my hand. "I haven't found anything like that. I wonder where they could be?"

I shrugged, tucked the keys in my pants pocket and sank onto a chair. "I have no idea. I checked her office and bedroom carefully and I didn't find it either. Could it have been in the library somewhere?"

She shook her head. "I cataloged every single book in there so the University could write us a receipt later. No diaries."

"No false books, huh?"

"Nothing like that at all. I'm sorry."

Kathy was still in the pantry boxing canned goods. "You girls all done upstairs?"

Betty nodded and pulled out a chair. "I do believe so. What's left here?"

"Just the kitchen and a bit of panty stuff. That's it. I'll be done with the pantry in a few minutes."

I glanced at the clock. Two-thirty meant I had a half hour before I'd have to dash out. "We put in a long day. You want to do the kitchen today or next week some time?" I pulled out my phone. One missed call. Damn. I'd never put the ring tone back on after the funeral yesterday.

Betty pushed a cold soda my way. "Next week is fine. Richard will be here and he may need something in the kitchen. I'm going to my own home tomorrow and I'm staying there a few days. I need to get away from here."

Kathy put her arms around Betty. "That's a very wise idea. This will wait another few days."

"That's how I figure it," she said. The fatigue showed on all of us. "I don't know how to thank you for all you've done for me. And for being friends to me, despite everything. I know I have not always been a pleasant person."

Kathy and I looked at each other over Betty's bent head. Her sorrow was now ours. During this horrible passage at least, she could count on people who'd protect her.

"It's okay, honey," Kathy crooned, the mother in her taking over. I finished my soda and stretched my aching back.

"Let's get that pantry emptied so you can drop the food off at the food bank, then we can head home." Kathy and I motioned Betty to sit still. "We can manage it. You take a break."

I moved in ahead of Kathy, climbed the short ladder and handed down the boxed pastas and a bag of flour. I reached into the corner to get the tin marked "sugar" and felt a latch on the panel behind the shelf. Even on my tiptoes I couldn't quite see the corner.

"Betty, do you have a flashlight handy?" I yelled from my perch on the step ladder.

Kathy clicked the button and handed it to me. Sure enough, there was a small stainless latch on the panel that hinged in the corner. I could make out a small door.

"I need a taller ladder," I called out from my perch.

"I don't have anything else. Maybe Kathy can help? She's a little taller than you are."

It was a point well made. Kathy raised a brow and made a shooing motion with her hands. I got out of the way, and she climbed up. She struggled for several minutes. Then we heard a grunt.

"What is it?" I asked wishing now that I was five eleven instead of five nine.

"Some kind of box," she mumbled, yanking the container free of its hiding place.

A chill ran down my spine and when Betty touched my arm, I almost jumped out of my skin. She jerked away from me.

"Sorry, Betty. I'm just over tired, I think."

She nodded. "Kathy, can you tell what you have there?"

"It's a metal box, looks pretty old. Has a tiny lock, too. I'll hand it to AJ."

I reached up to take it from her. It was an old strong box, generally used to hold things like wills, deeds, and papers like that. The instant I saw the lock, I knew I had the key.

Betty helped Kathy off the ladder, and we met at Matilda's kitchen table. I pulled the keys from my pocket and looked at her. "This is yours, Betty. Maybe you should open it?"

She began to shake. "I want to throw it out in the dumpster without opening it at all." Tears filled her eyes again. "You take it with you. Maybe it will help you find why she was killed. I don't want to see what you find."

I put the keys back in my pocket and moved the box to the chair by my purse and jacket.

She nodded and let out a breath. "Okay. Now get out of here before you're late for court."

I stared at the dusty metal box and sighed. It had been in that pantry wall for many years. I supposed it wouldn't hurt anything if it kept its secrets for another few hours.

# CHAPTER SIXTEEN

I took the world's fastest shower, slipped into a black pleated skirt and a sweater, and then pulled on my boots.

My father, smart fellow he is, stayed out of my way, handing me my brief bag and coat on the way through the kitchen.

"Travis called while you were in the shower. The judge is running late and will see you all at four o'clock."

"Thank goodness," I breathed, kissing his cheek. I nodded in the direction of the metal box on the kitchen table. "Would you put that in my office on the desk, please?"

He nodded and I flew out the door, headed for the Putnam County Courthouse. I didn't want to be late, even if I was more than likely just an extraneous witness to the proceedings.

***

Margie Donovan had on a pale blue pantsuit, a simple haircut which framed her thin face and a pink lipstick that worked well with her auburn hair and pale, freckled complexion. I arrived in time to give her a hug and my husband a quick kiss.

We were escorted into the judge's cramped chambers. I smelled old books and lemon furniture polish.

"Mrs. Donovan, please take a seat by the bailiff," Judge Fishburne instructed her. He waited until she was settled before acknowledging the two attorneys who faced his huge oak desk.

"Gentlemen, we've been discussing a plea agreement for this case, is that correct?" The stenographer typed away on his special computer. "For the record, please state your name and position in this case."

"I, Travis Buchanan, attorney for the defendant Marguerite Donovan, have requested that the court accept a plea of guilty to involuntary manslaughter and a suspended sentence for that action." He turned to the State's Attorney standing beside him.

"I, State's Attorney Joshua Broward, have agreed to accept a guilty plea for the charge of involuntary manslaughter. I am not in agreement on the sentence, Your Honor."

"I see," said the judge. "Mr. Buchanan. Why do you believe this action should not be considered voluntary manslaughter?"

"Your Honor, this case borders on self-defense, but it is clearly not voluntary manslaughter. Mrs. Donovan had every reason to believe her husband was going to inflict bodily harm on her, yet again. She was unwilling to allow that and sought to intimidate him into not hurting her."

"And how did she seek to intimidate him?"

"Mrs. Donovan pulled Mr. Donovan's handgun from the nightstand and held it in a threatening manner hoping to dissuade him from hitting her. He had already hurt her extensively that same evening."

Broward cleared his throat. "Your Honor, although I do not believe that Mrs. Donovan was actually *planning* to shoot her husband dead that evening, she was acting with malice. She had to be. He had injured her many times over the years. Involuntary manslaughter requires that her actions be without malice. She should have called the police, not held him at gun point."

"Understood, Mr. Broward," said the judge. "Mr. Buchanan, what is your reasoning for petitioning for this lesser charge?"

"The sentencing, Your Honor. I believe that Margie Donovan and her children have paid enough. And for the record, I do not believe that a self-defense mentality requires malice at all."

"Mr. Broward, you both have valid arguments. And we have discussed two separate sentences. Since we are in agreement on the circumstances of Mr. Donovan's death, I'd like to speak with Mrs. Donovan before I prepare sentence."

Travis moved aside to allow the bailiff to escort Margie to the chair in front of the judge's desk. He nodded at her but stopped short of a smile.

"Mrs. Donovan, are you entering a guilty plea for the death of your husband, of your own free will?"

Her hands visibly shaking, she looked at him. "I am, Your Honor."

"And did you, of your own accord, remove his gun from the drawer and hold it in a menacing manner?"

"I did, sir."

"Did you intend to kill your husband that night, Mrs. Donovan?"

"No sir."

"At any time, Mrs. Donovan, did you ever think about killing your husband?"

"Yes, sir."

His brows raised, he glanced at Travis and Broward before continuing. "Would you please explain, Mrs. Donovan?"

"My husband was a cruel man, Your Honor. I thought about killing him many times, but I didn't want to go to jail. I ran away a half dozen times, but he always found me and things got worse. I thought about killing myself too, but couldn't do it. I couldn't leave my kids, your honor. Who would take care of them?"

The judge wrote in silence for several minutes, the only sound was the ticking of the large-faced clock on the wall and the scratching sound of his writing. When he put down his pen, he nodded to the bailiff.

"All rise," the bailiff announced.

Everyone but the court reporter stood at attention. "Mrs. Donovan, your plea of guilty is accepted by this court. You are hereby considered guilty of involuntary manslaughter in the death of your husband, Brian Donovan. In accordance with Title 18, Section 1112 of the United States Code, you can be sentenced to a fine of up to twenty-thousand dollars and up to six years in prison."

He stopped to allow that information to sink in. He looked at both attorneys, but they carefully maintained no expression.

"Therefore, it is my decision that you not be fined, but instead be sentenced to six months in jail and four years probation. Since you have already served six months while awaiting your trial, your jail time is hereby considered complete. You will have forty-eight hours to meet with the probation department."

It was all I could do not to jump to my feet and cheer. Instead, I worked to remain quiet and respectful as is expected in a judge's chambers.

"Your Honor, if I may?" Travis spoke after clearing his throat.

"Yes, Counselor?"

"If it would please the Court, Mrs. Donovan's children are temporarily in the custody of her mother who lives in Mobile, Alabama. We feel it is dangerous for Mrs. Donovan to remain in Florida due to threats received by Mr. Donovan's extended family. Would it be possible for her to serve her probation in Alabama?"

"I have no objection to that if the State has none. Mr. Broward, how does the State feel about this request?"

"We will agree to that as long as the probation is coordinated with the State of Florida, Your Honor."

The judge raised his gavel. "So be it. That needs to be completed in the next 72 hours, gentlemen." He banged the gavel on the desk. "The case of the People of the State of Florida versus Donovan is hereby concluded. Thank you all."

As the judge stood to leave chambers, the bailiff crossed the room and spoke to him. He turned to the attorneys.

"Gentlemen, it would seem that our local media hounds are waiting outside for your exit. You may want to use the alternate means unless you need the publicity."

Travis and I moved toward Margie Donovan at the same time. She stood her ground, chin held high.

"I'm a free woman, am I not?" she asked in a strong voice. When Travis nodded, she smiled at him.

"Then I'll walk out the front door like a free woman. No more shame for me."

Travis took his briefcase and caught up with her in three long strides.

"Margie, there's no telling who's in that crowd out there. If Bobby Joe or another relative is out there, your pride could get you killed. You said you wanted to make sure you were there for your kids. That means not doing stupid things."

She looked at him, defiance in every muscle of her body. Travis stood still, waiting for her decision. Being married to me, he sure knew how to handle a stubborn woman. But no matter what door she used, he would be at her side. She didn't look at me.

"Then get me out of here, Mr. Buchanan. I've truly come to hate this place."

We walked to the secured elevator and made our way through the corridor that led to the courthouse administrative building. Travis pushed open the door and held it for Margie. They both breathed in the fresh air as though they'd been holding their breath for hours.

I felt like a kid, grinning from ear to ear with their victory. He turned to me.

"Meet you at home, honey?"

I nodded and reached around him to give Margie a hug. "I'm so glad you are free today. This is the best thing we could have hoped for."

Tears filled Margie's eyes. "I want to call my mom and kids. They'll be waiting to hear something."

I handed her my cell phone and stepped to the side, keeping her between me and Travis, but not exactly within earshot.

"I'm going to get her a train ticket home. We can hit the Café for some dinner," he said.

Margie handed my phone back. "Thank you, Travis for all you've done. I can't tell you how wonderful it is to be free. But I was always sure I would be, you know."

He smiled. "I'm glad you had faith. And I'm glad this could be handled this way. You and your children will need time to mend now."

She looked away but remained quiet. "Why don't we stop and pick up some dinner, my treat. It's the least I can do to repay all you've both done for me."

I shrugged. "That's not necessary, but if it will make you happy, that's fine with me. I'll see you guys a little later, then." I had a mystery box I wanted to get home and open.

I watched as Travis held open the passenger door of his truck for Margie, helped her inside, then strode around to his side, tossed in his briefcase, and waved in my direction.

173

We concentrated on getting to St. John's Avenue, away from the television trucks and people milling about waiting to catch a glimpse of an exonerated killer.

I took a deep breath and let it out. They turned north on Highway 17, and I went south.

***

"Papa?" I called when I got home, wondering where he'd gone. In the kitchen there was a flashing light on the small LCD screen he'd mounted under the cabinet. I touched the screen and his face and voice popped into view.

"I'm across the street at Mrs. Macomber's house. She asked me to look at her citrus trees. I'll be back later."

*Hmm.* I shrugged out of my jacket and hung it and my purse on the hooks by the door. My father needed friends his age and Mrs. Macomber had been a widow for almost ten years. At least he was finally out of the house. He'd almost sequestered himself since he'd arrived, and I wasn't beyond worrying about him.

I changed into my jeans and a turquoise *ANGEL INVESTIGATIONS* sweatshirt, pulled a comb through my hair and went back downstairs.

The metal box from the Renkin house was just where I asked Papa to put it. Just as I poured a tall glass of lemonade, I heard the heavy crunch of Travis's truck

174

tires on the driveway gravel. I pushed through the screen door and jogged out to meet them.

I pulled open his door and wrapped my arms around his waist. "Welcome home, Victorious Warriors."

Margie smiled at me and then undid her seatbelt. "My train leaves at eight-thirty, so I'll only impose on your hospitality for a short while. Thank you so much for all you've done."

I walked around to her side of the truck and opened the door. She handed me a plastic restaurant bag that smelled suspiciously like smoked ribs and moved to step down from the cab. I heard a truck approaching fast and turned to see who it might be.

I saw the rifle barrel hanging out the window.

"Get down," I shouted, pushing Margie back into the truck.

Still turned toward the street, I saw the flash and then I don't remember a thing.

# CHAPTER SEVENTEEN

"AJ," called someone from very far away. Even with my eyes closed, the antiseptic smell was too familiar to dismiss.

"Travis, where are you?" I croaked.

"Right here, honey. You're going to be all right, but you need to stay still."

"Margie?"

"She's okay. You took the bullet meant for her."

Shane Davis stood beside Travis. "We'll have Bobby Joe Fletcher in custody shortly."

My mouth felt like a stale rice cake, and I tried to lick my lips, but even that hurt. "How long... did Margie get home to her kids?"

"She's on her way, thanks to you. She should be just about there, by now."

"How bad is this?"

"You've got guardian angels, Trouble. The bullet got you in the chest, nicked a couple of ribs, went out your shoulder, and lodged in the door of the truck. You're going to be sore as hell for a few weeks, but doctors say you'll be okay. Bullet didn't hit anything vital."

As my vision cleared, I glanced at Travis, who looked like hell. "Vital to whom?" I asked. "I'm okay. You look like you could use some sleep. Why don't you go home and rest? You can bring my father back with you later."

"Are you kidding? Until they catch Fletcher, I'm not leaving you for an instant. Although it would seem my being around isn't going to keep you safe after all." He rubbed his face with his hands. "I could use a nap, though. And your father is here, somewhere."

Deputy Davis cleared his throat. "We'll keep someone posted here until he's in custody, Travis. Obviously, the restraining order was ineffectual."

"Usually is," I muttered, remembering the stories of women whose beatings got worse after issuing the useless, but required piece of paper.

"That's true, but because of it, the penalties are so much more enforceable," he said. Travis nodded in agreement.

My father joined us carrying a cardboard tray full of coffee containers. "So, how is my daughter this morning?" His careful cheeriness made me want to cry, but I was really just too tired.

"I'm fine, Papa. Sore."

"I'm not surprised, Antonia. Bullets do a great deal of damage to the body."

"Did you see what happened? Do we really know it was Bobby Joe?" I asked.

"I was having tea with Mrs. Macomber when I saw Travis pull up. I wanted to know how things turned out, so I just started out the door to come home, when the black Ford pulled up. After the shooting, he sped off, but I got his license plate."

"That only means it was his truck, doesn't necessarily mean it was him," Deputy Davis pointed out. "There are still a lot of unanswered questions in this case. We have enough to pick him up for questioning, though."

I looked at Shane Davis and nodded at him. "What else is eating at you?"

"There's something you should know, AJ."

I searched his rugged face for a clue. "I'm not going to like this, am I?"

He shook his head. "No, and I don't either. We think we found your homeless guy yesterday afternoon."

"Please don't tell me Sarge is dead. He could be the only lead we have about who Matilda was with at the mill."

The Deputy stayed quiet and looked at the floor.

"Shit, how did it happen?"

"He was hit by a train. Suicide, maybe. We know he was *not* exactly stable. It happens far too often with our homeless guys."

Travis squeezed my hand, my father nodded at me, and I just let go. Too tired. Far too tired for any more death.

I closed my eyes and let the tears fall where they would.

\*\*\*

I slept for more than eleven hours. When I woke up, I felt like *I'd* been hit by a train. Travis was reading in the chair by the window when I called to him.

"Well, if it isn't my hero," I said, winking at him.

He took off his reading glasses. "You're the hero, lady. Do you need anything?"

"I need a drink and then I want to go home."

He moved to the bedside table and poured me some water. Holding the straw to my lips, he gave me a small drink of water. It was the best water I'd ever tasted, sulfur and all.

"You can't go home today. If you don't show any infection and can get up and around this afternoon, you can go home tomorrow."

"Judging by the sun, it must already be afternoon, right?"

"Almost two. Let me get the nurse, then you can get up."

I'd have protested except that I hurt too much. If he wanted to play nursemaid, it was fine with me.

"Mrs. Buchanan," the young woman with an RN tag began. "How do you feel?"

I explained the aches and pains I could locate, then asked if I could get up to go to the bathroom.

"I'm going to remove your IV, and if your husband will be so kind as to assist you so you don't fall on your pretty face, you may use the bathroom. Then you can sit up for little while. I'll go get you something light to eat."

I waited while she removed the needles and lines, then bandaged my left arm. She looked down at me. "That rib is going to hurt bad, even with the pain killers. Move very slowly and let your husband help you actually stand, okay?"

She stepped aside to allow Travis bedside. He put out his arm so I could leverage myself at my own pace, then supported me to a sitting position. I gasped for air.

"Take it slowly, Mrs. Buchanan. You'll feel a bit better when you are cleaned up and have something in your stomach."

I nodded, unable to speak. In Quantico, I'd been zapped by stun guns and blasted with plastic bullets, and they'd hurt like hell. Almost all of my FBI physical training had hurt like hell. But this was a new caliber of pain. The type that made me think of lightning bolts

180

shooting through a Northern Pine tree and firing straight out the outstretched limbs. Good Lord Almighty.

"I've got you, babe," Travis whispered.

I swung my feet to the floor, and he helped me to stand. Good thing; at the rate the room was spinning, I'd have been kissing those pretty blue and white floor tiles.

The nurse left us with a promise to return shortly. I smiled at Travis, and he winced. "Okay, so I've had better days," I growled.

"Haven't we all," he muttered as he maneuvered me into the bathroom.

Thanks to a seat in the walk-in shower and modern technology, I got a decent shower and felt better by the minute. In my own pajamas and sitting in a large chair eating broth and crackers, I figured I was just about on top of the world.

***

Deputy Davis returned with my father, right around six p.m. and both looked pleased to see me, so I must have looked better. Travis was asleep in the empty bed next to me, showered, fed, and exhausted.

My father pulled up a chair and sat next to me, a folded sheet of paper in his hand. "We aren't out of the woods yet. You got another poem last night." He shook open the paper and read it to us.

*You dig and you dig for things you don't know, but the Sarge is now dead and you're next to go.*

I looked at Davis. "I hope they're doing an autopsy on the poor guy. I'll bet he was dead when the train hit him. And someone in the Sheriff's Office is giving the killer their information."

"You think?" Travis said, suddenly awake, swinging his feet to the floor.

"Yes, they'll do an autopsy," the deputy said, "But, you know it'll be a few days." He shifted his feet. "It isn't me who's leaking anything. We're now limiting who has access to the case."

"I guess that's good. God, I have to get home and open Matilda's hidden box."

"What's that?" they all asked in unison.

I filled them in with the highpoints.

Travis looked at Shawn and Papa. "You two make sure that box is safe at the house. It might hold the answers to this whole thing, or it might not, but I don't want anything happening to it."

The two men nodded and turned to go. "Deputy?" I asked, "Have you picked up Bobby Joe yet?"

"No, ma'am, we haven't. Nobody's seen him in a couple of days."

"He'll be the next one we find dead. I wonder what the tie in is between him and the Renkin family."

"I don't know. Donovan and Fletcher grew up in Gainesville and you folks are from the Creek. Doesn't mean there isn't a connection, I just haven't put the pieces together yet. We'll leave an officer by the door until we do, though."

"Can he be trusted?"

Deputy Davis looked at us. "I sure hope so. I'm thinking the connection is someone much older. Someone on the force a long time. This officer's only been with us five years and I can't find any family ties to what's happening."

I guess I had to be happy with that. And the fact that my husband was packing his Glock.

# CHAPTER EIGHTEEN

"You go stretch out on the couch. I'll get the box from your office." Travis dropped my backpack at the foot of the stairs and gently pushed me forward.

A short while later, fortified with a pain killer and a cup of hot tea, I settled into the living room in front of the fire, the sturdy old box between my thighs. Travis sat behind me on the sofa. My father occupied an overstuffed wing chair by the bookcase near the window. Pain was now a distant memory.

"The keys were in my pants pocket," I said. He left to retrieve my bloodied jeans and returned with the keys in the palm of his hand.

"Too bad Shane couldn't be here."

"He's got to sleep sometime, AJ. He said he'd call when he got on duty this afternoon."

I tried the larger key and it slipped into the rusty keyhole like butter. The tiny "click" resounded in the room and I held my breath. I lifted the lid and found another box. Jeesh. What the hell was Matilda doing?

The inside box had no hasp or lock. I lifted it out and placed the lock-box on the floor. I pulled the lid off the interior box and stared at the leather-bound journal inside. *Richard A. Renkin* gleamed on the cover in twenty-four carat gold.

Hell, I was sure it would have been Matilda's book. *Ah, well.* I placed the smaller key into the hole and unlocked the strap that held the book secured. I flipped open the book to begin reading.

The journal, written in Richard's strong handwriting, started after Betty arrived in the Renkin family. Clearly a textbook sociopath, the man was totally bereft of emotion or conscience. I was not at all surprised in the man's level of hypocrisy, but I got a chill anyway.

The entries were not daily or even weekly. Instead, they were rather sporadic, a purging he seemed to need once in a while. Three months after Betty was born, November nineteenth to be exact, he wrote several pages, some legible, some not. I read aloud.

*"I finally fired Mesters. His insolence and disrespect cannot be tolerated any longer. He has no right to speak to me about how I treat the women in my family. They are mine to do with as I please."*

*Why did that sound familiar to me?*

Richard made it perfectly clear that Nathan could support Matilda and the child if he so desired, but Richard would not do anything more than society dictated that he must. He also promised Nathan that he would ruin Matilda and her daughter publicly if Nathan interfered. Renkin was really quite the bastard.

*"Mesters folded like a cheap suitcase,"* he wrote, his penmanship quite clear and bold. *"He should kill me for this, but he's gutless, so he won't. He'll protect that wimp of a woman, even if it kills him. I sincerely hope that it does."*

I shut the book and pushed it away. The chills were worse, and I sipped at my tea, willing it to calm me down.

"Pretty ugly stuff, honey. It's amazing that Betty has any normal genes at all," Travis offered as he gently massaged the tension in my neck.

"I talked with her yesterday. She grew up in a house of horrors, Travis."

My father looked crushed. "I did not know about this cruelty. He was crass and disrespectful to others, but I never suspected this. I like to think we'd have done something about it if we'd known."

I smiled at him. "I know you and Mama would have, Papa."

The book was perhaps three-hundred pages in total. I flipped through. Major events, family gatherings, holidays seemed to trigger Richard's need to write. Each entry was a bit more direct, angrier, and pettier. He delighted in whatever disgrace he could bestow upon his wife and daughter. True to his promise to Nathan, he never once acknowledged Betty as his daughter. Not in word, nor deed. His entries certainly made it clear why she felt her father hated her so much. It had to have hurt terribly. I know I would have died without my father's love and approval.

Very few entries mentioned his son, perhaps because he found no fault with his male heir?

The last entry by Richard was written a week before he died:

> *I spoke with Matilda tonight, for the first time in weeks. The child will graduate from college in a few months, and I want them both out of my house. She was completely unreasonable of course, claiming that the house is hers, not mine, and that I should leave. She's too stupid to understand_that her father gave her to me. She has nothing that isn't mine. I'll kill her if she doesn't leave.*

Whoa. The mantle clock chimed twelve times and I sat back and listened to the tones echo through the quiet. My eyes were burning like I'd poured alcohol in them and the muscles in my neck, right between my shoulder blades, were on fire.

"How about we finish this tomorrow?" Travis asked half-heartedly.

"I won't sleep with all this on my mind, so no sense in leaving it unfinished," I said.

Travis's hand resting on the back of my neck helped me to continue.

Several pages were blank, and then another entry appeared. This handwriting was nearly perfect with its loops and evenly spaced letters. The same hand had written this entry that had written me my retainer check two weeks ago.

Matilda had picked up where Richard had left off. That also meant that she'd read his mean, gloating entries with her own eyes. I continued reading to Travis and my father.

> *Richard was a truly evil man. I can't understand why my father would ever have thought he would be good for me or the family business. Although I do not deserve the Lord's help after what I've done, I'm grateful for the diabetes. Fool injected himself with saline. He will never wake up again and my Betty is finally safe.*

My head was buzzing. Matilda had killed Richard. "Thank goodness it was Matilda, Travis, because officer of the court or not, I'd have put the damned journal in the fire if it had been Betty who'd killed old man Renkin."

There was no entry for the day they buried Richard Renkin Sr. Everyone had probably been dancing in the parlor. Well, all but Richard Jr., I guess.

Betty's graduation day. A photo in her cap and gown, a beaming Matilda and a thin, but dashing, Nathan Mesters, standing on either side. A proud day, for sure. Dora was conspicuously absent from the happy family photo, just as Betty had said.

Journal entry, day after graduation:

> *Nathan's cancer is progressing faster than we thought it would. God has blessed me with Nate's love and support these years and I'm glad he could see my lovely daughter reach her dreams. I think I was still hoping that he'd be cured and we could sell the properties and go away together. My heart is breaking. In a matter of months, he will be dead. What will I do without him?*

I felt the tears start. Hell, this woman didn't have a single ounce of good luck. *Shit*. I swallowed around the lump in my throat, sniffed, and wiped my face with my sleeve. Through blurry eyes I turned the page. Travis began to read beside me.

> *Nathan's ashes were buried today. I've cried so hard and so long that I don't have any tears left. Poor Dora is the one*

*to mourn, though. She's never had a chance. The incestuous union of our father and his twin sister have ensured she is quite insane. Then her only child, a beautiful daughter, is torn from her life without warning. I married the man she adored and loved the man she married. We'll all have a lovely time in Hell, I suppose.*

*But Betty is safe and happy. She's met a nice young man and he adores her. Both Dora and I want that for her. She's terribly upset over Nathan's death, believing I'm sure, that he was her real father. Should I have told her the awful truth?*

I sucked in a breath. How much misery could be attributed to dirty family secrets? Were they really, truly secrets anymore?

Casual, lonesome entries about the gardens during their change of season, the bake sale in town, her first grandchildren, Richard's two, complete with photos. I resumed reading.

*Richard is not as hostile with his father gone. He is wonderful with his babies. I can only hope he will be happy with his*

*family. There is no other reason to live,*
*but to keep them safe and see them happy.*

Betty's wedding, with a couple of stunning photos, was worth ten whole pages. A proud and happy mother gushing over her beautiful daughter and handsome son-in-law. Michael looked at Betty with such adoration that a lump lodged in my throat again. Thinking to the funeral service, I realized that he still looked at her that way. Dora obviously did not know how much Betty was loved by the man.

"Matilda had some very happy days. I'm glad for that. So much of her life was miserable," Travis said softly. "The imbalance reminds me of my parents, some. My father wasn't evil or anything, but my mother was definitely a walking widow. I doubt my father saw a single one of my baseball games. But my mom was always there, as though she could make up for his absences."

I covered his hand with mine. "He thought he was doing the right thing for his family, though. Had your parents not been killed in that plane crash, I'm sure he'd have spent all his time catching up, Travis."

"Goes to show, you can't wait to do those things. He left me very well off financially, but as a kid, I'd have given everything I had to have my dad in the stands at a game."

191

I understood all too well what a child wishes for in the face of life's harshest blows.

I thumbed through the book. No entries until the very last page. An epitaph, perhaps?

Travis leaned over my shoulder. "*My sister called me this evening*," he read.

I noticed the date. *Hotdamn!* She'd written this the Thursday before she'd disappeared.

I struggled off the sofa as the clock chimed two and began to pace while I read. "Listen to this," I whispered.

> *She wants to see me about Betty. I told her weeks ago I was going to Arizona. I suspect with me leaving the area, she wants a chance to reveal the truth. I find that I no longer care, but will it hurt our beautiful daughter? I don't think she should. It's a selfish thing to do. We are such miserable women, we Mayfields. Not at all like our fun-loving ancestors with their brothels and horse racing. I will have to convince her to leave Betty alone.*
>
> *It's time that this charade is over. Richard Jr. has made some terrible mistakes, but in speaking with him yesterday, I believe he's learned from them. My Betty is happy with her Michael. I am more tired of living than any human being should be with all that life*

*could have been. Antonia will finish the*
*history for me, so that people will remember*
*the good that the Mayfield's once did for*
*this precious piece of Florida. I'll sell this*
*old mausoleum and relocate with Richard if*
*he'll still have me.*

That was it. I closed the book and laid it on the mantle. Had Matilda willingly walked into her own death?

Travis started to close the lid of the box, then stopped. "There's something else in this box, AJ."

He handed me a yellowed envelope which I opened with care. A carefully folded birth certificate, brandishing the seal of the Great State of Florida, bore the name of Betty Jean Renkin.

The other document was a medical claim in the name of Matilda Renkin, dated the year that Richard Junior was born.

Matilda Renkin had almost died giving birth to her son. The only thing that had saved her life was a hysterectomy.

## CHAPTER NINETEEN

"Do you understand what this means?" I said to Travis, gingerly settling back onto the sofa.

"Betty can't be Matilda's daughter. The birth certificate was either falsified or the wrong mother's name was provided to the hospital."

"Well, this stinks. I'd bet my life that she doesn't know this. And if she isn't Matilda's daughter, who is her *real* mother?" My head felt like it weighed a hundred pounds. "Oh, damn. I really, really hate this."

Travis took my hand in his. "Why don't you see if you can put together a family tree that we can count on. We won't say anything to her unless we have to and until we know the whole truth."

"Good idea. I'm going to bed, maybe you can put this away where it will be safe."

My father came to my side. "I will put away the book. Travis will put you to bed. You must rest, Antonia."

The next morning at breakfast, there was an odd silence. I looked around at my father and Travis and put my fork down. My eggs would have to wait.

"What's up with you two?" I asked, reaching gingerly for my orange juice glass.

"I figured I'd put the wash in for you. Found this in your jacket pocket. Want to explain?"

Travis held up a small bundle of papers that had been torn into quarters. The outer paper was the memorial program from Matilda's funeral. Inside were newspaper clippings.

"I found them in the trash basket beside Dora's desk. I thought I'd get to go through them when I got home, but it was so late, I guess I forgot."

"This isn't admissible evidence, you know. She didn't give it to you and you stole it from her home," Travis said, running a hand through his hair.

"And you and I both know even if Dora's behind the threats, no jury is going to convict her of anything. She denied being at the funeral, but I recognized the program. I didn't get to look at the clippings, but I planned on going through them."

Both men stayed silent, so apparently, they had examined whatever was contained inside the program. My father spoke first.

"I taped the papers back together. The account of Fletcher's arrest and threats against you was one of the clippings. Another was the announcement of the pending sale of the mill property. Still another was of the Donovan trial date announcement."

I pushed away my breakfast. "She was stalking us *all*?"

"In a way, I suppose you could say that." Travis said, pushing my plate back to me. "Eat."

"I don't want to eat. I want to know what's going on. And don't you think someone should warn Betty that her crazy aunt is on the loose?"

"I talked with Michael. He intends to keep Betty busy and if that doesn't work, he's taking her to the Bahamas for a few days. She'll be safe. You can do the research magic that you do and when we know something for sure, you can figure out what she'll need to know. But first you need to eat."

\*\*\*

I had no problem avoiding Betty. I spent the next three days mending. The rib would take a long time, but I was working the shoulder gently to help relieve the stiffness. The hot tub helped a great deal, as did Travis's careful hands.

Psycho-poet had not sent a fourth poem to me, making me wonder if he or she didn't know I was home from the hospital. That might mean the leak had been plugged at the Sheriff's office, or there was simply nothing new to taunt me about. However, the poem hadn't even mentioned the shooting though it was in every paper from the Panhandle to Key West.

That had me thinking that the attack on us was about Margie going free and not about the Renkin case. Bobby Joe Fletcher was still at large, or dead, but at any rate, had not been located yet. And on this glorious, unseasonably warm Sunday, I was feeling stronger and excited about baking for Thanksgiving which was only five days away. Hard to believe that it had only been ten days since I'd discovered Matilda dead in the mill.

"You should probably still use that sling, AJ," my father suggested when he saw me in the kitchen taking inventory of my baking supplies.

"I will, Papa. I have to use the arm a little bit, though. I don't start physical therapy for two weeks yet and the stiffness is terrible."

"Don't overdo it, that's all," interjected Travis who was headed for the coffee pot.

"Yes dears," I sneered, wishing they'd both stop fussing over me like giant mother hens.

"Do you want to go buy some pumpkins and squash today, maybe?" Travis offered.

"Sure. Any word from Margie?"

"She called Friday. She has to see her probation officer tomorrow morning. She's very happy to be back with her kids, as you can imagine. Wanted to know how you're doing."

"I hope you told her everything's fine with us. They're going to have a great Thanksgiving, aren't they?"

He laughed. "Sure are. As are we. We are very blessed that you weren't killed."

My father grunted in agreement.

My heart skipped a beat and I sighed. "I know, I know. It's really bothering me that they haven't picked up Bobby Joe, though."

"He knows this area well; he could be hiding anywhere. I'm relieved that we haven't found him dead on the front porch or something, that's all I can say." Travis finished his coffee.

"Maybe we'll have information on Sarge tomorrow. That would make me feel better. If they can identify him, his family can lay him to rest with dignity. A soldier deserves that at the very least."

Travis cleared his throat. "He's been identified. His name is Staff Sargeant Earl MacClellan. US Army, 153rd Infantry Division. Served three tours in Viet Nam. Lost his brother there. Born in Birmingham, Alabama."

"Well, now he can go home."

"This will have to be home for him. He doesn't have any family that could be located. His parents died while he was in Viet Nam and his wife and twin daughters were killed in a car wreck in Texas seventeen years ago."

"He's been wandering since, I'll bet. Can he be buried here in one of our Veteran's cemeteries? Or can we make the arrangements for him?"

"He was discharged with honors in 1973. Shane's contacted our local congresswoman to make that happen."

I nodded. I still wanted to know what he'd seen if anything. Would anyone show up at his burial beside us and Deputy Shane?

In my head I could hear bagpipes and the gun salute. Sergeant McClellan deserved that at the very least.

\*\*\*

We spent the better part of Sunday cutting up pumpkins and squash for pie, while I worried about what to do about Betty.

My father was an artist in his own right with his tiny knife and intricate designs. He carved a beautiful spread-tail turkey for the dining room table. Neither my shoulder nor my right side would tolerate putting my effort into sculpting or scooping, but I was able to at least puree the flesh of the vegetables and get it ready for baking.

"My goodness, gracious," Mrs. Macomber said, knocking on the kitchen door. "Should you be doing all of this, young lady?" she chided me.

I laughed. "I'm not doing much, I assure you. These able-bodied males are doing all the hard work." I motioned for her to sit down and join us. "Can I get you a glass of tea or make you something hot?"

"Bless your heart, but no. I wanted to tell you something, though. I got a call from Ethel Southerland this afternoon. She's been in Ohio visiting her daughter for the past three weeks."

My father took the pail of scraps out the door and set it on the porch. "Who is Ethel Southerland?" he asked.

"She lives in the only other house on the street where Matilda Renkin's place is. She didn't know that Matilda had died until I told her today."

The hair on the back of my neck stood up. "Does she know something?"

"Well, she said when she was packing for her trip, a gold Cadillac was in Matilda's driveway. It was gone by the time Ethel went to bed, though."

Travis looked at me. "I'll call Davis and let him know."

Mrs. Macomber smiled. "Did that help you?"

Travis took her hands in his and kissed her cheek. "You may have helped more than you know, Mrs. Macomber."

"Why, Yankee, you are full of yourself, aren't you?"

He bowed and smiled, then excused himself to call Shane.

My father walked Mrs. Macomber home and my cell phone rang. "AJ, this is Betty. I don't know if you're feeling up to it, but Richard's at the house. You said you wanted to talk to him."

"Did he come from Gainesville?"

"I didn't ask him. He arrived in Florida last night and drove to mother's this morning. But he seemed to be calm. Might be a good time to see him."

"Okay, maybe I'll do that." After assuring each other that we were both doing fine, we hung up. She still sounded exhausted, and I was glad she hadn't offered to drive down from Orange Park.

Travis came into the office and sat on the loveseat. "Shane wasn't there, so I left a message on his cell phone instead of at the station." He rested his forearms on his knees. "Who was on your phone?"

"Betty. Richard's at Matilda's right now. I want to go talk to him. He's still an unknown factor and I think we need to do this. Will you drive me over there?"

He kissed my nose. "I'd do anything for you, Trouble. Leave your dad a note about where we're going, and I'll go get my keys."

\*\*\*

Lights burned in several windows at Matilda's. A 2008 Pontiac G6 sat in the driveway, the standard rental car for most of the State of Florida.

I was only slightly disappointed that it wasn't a borrowed Cadillac. Travis pressed the bell and we waited.

The door opened, and Richard stood barefooted, aged, and bent. His forty-nine years hadn't been kind to him, either.

"Richard? I'm Antonia Buchanan, Betty's friend. This is my husband, Travis."

He moved aside to let us into the foyer. "Thank you for helping Betty with all of this. I tried to get here sooner, but I had business meetings planned and there didn't seem to be much I could accomplish by rushing here."

Travis stood close by me, doing his best not to look confrontational. "It was a nice service. I'm sure the U.S. Marshal's office would have allowed you to come."

At about six foot one, Richard was only slightly shorter than Travis. His dark brown hair was streaked with silver and his eyes were the color of chocolate. His shoulders slumped forward a bit more.

"So, you know about my legal issues." He motioned us to the living room, and we sat on the antiques that now sported Lucy's day-glow orange appraisal tags.

"I guess everyone knows about my legal issues." He sighed. "Quite a mess I made of following my father's example. Anyway, Betty said you might want to talk to me. You're here, so what do you want?"

"Were you here November 9th when your mother was killed?"

"Killed?" he said, his eyes snapping open. "Nobody told me she was killed. Do you know that for sure?"

Travis put his hands palm to palm and rested his elbows on jean-clad thighs. "Your mother wasn't a diabetic, Richard. Yet her blood sugar was high enough to kill her. What's your guess?"

All the color drained out of his face. "I didn't know any of that." He cleared his throat. "I wasn't here two weeks ago. I haven't been in this house in a good number of years."

"I didn't mean 'here' as in this house. I'm referring to your flight into Gainesville and the rental car you picked up in Palatka. How'd you get from Gainesville to Palatka, Richard?" I asked.

"Are you accusing me of killing my own mother?"

"Did you?" I snapped. Travis put his hand over mine.

"No," Junior growled. "That's absurd. We weren't close, but I was trying to change that. I've made a lot of terrible mistakes that I'm sorry for. I wanted her to come live with me and leave this god-forsaken place."

"You still didn't answer my question," I pushed again.

"One of my Aunt Dora's friends drove me. He was attending some law enforcement seminar."

I fought the urge to look at Travis.

"Did you stay with your Aunt Dora?" Travis asked.

"I was going to, that's why I didn't reserve a rental car in Gainesville. Hell, Dora has two perfectly good cars. I was supposed to use one of hers when I arrived. I called her a half-dozen times, but she never answered the phone. When Lt. Barnes showed up for me, I figured it beat taking the bus all the way to Chastity Creek."

"You didn't stay with Dora, and you didn't stay with your mother. Where'd you stay?" I asked.

"At the Quality Inn on the river. Left in the morning for the airport."

"Did you see your mother at all that trip?" Travis asked.

Richard shook his head. "I was determined to convince her to come to Arizona. She'd changed her mind and I didn't know why. I drove by here three times but then I left. I didn't even call her. I returned to Gainesville the next day and flew home." He shifted his feet.

I wasn't getting it. "Okay, you dodged the marshals, flew from Arizona to Florida and back again and didn't see a single member of your family?"

"You can believe me or not, I don't give a damn. But that's the truth."

"Well," I conceded. "It's easy enough to confirm. You were either on a plane or you weren't."

## CHAPTER TWENTY

Since I was pretty much restricted to desk-type activities for the time being, the genealogy project became top priority. Thankful to the various services I subscribed to, some of the information I wanted was readily available. There are few tools as comprehensive for locating people, as genealogy services. Those and on-line newspapers.

Although midwives are still a popular practice in the south, I wasn't sure I'd find all the pieces, but at least I'd have a good start on things. Midwives were required to report births, but it wasn't always done, at least prior to the mid 1900's, with the formation of formal counties.

As it turned out, Dora was the firstborn daughter of Anna and Joshua Mayfield, both first generation Americans. The children of immigrants who arrived from Scotland and Ireland through the Port of New Orleans, they were both born in the Tallahassee area. Joshua had a twin sister named Sarah, but there seemed to be no siblings for Anna.

Matilda had been born in 1933, two years after Dora. Matilda was born in a hospital; Dora had been born at home. Their mother Anna died in 1942 of consumption. Dora would have been eleven.

Anna Mayfield's father died in a farming accident in Ocala, November 1930, so he'd never met his granddaughters. No Florida records existed for Anna's mother or either of Joshua's parents. Joshua's sister Sarah died at home, the day after Dora was born. Poor Joshua, I thought.

I paid for a search of cemetery records and sat back to consider the information I had.

I didn't know what all the family dynamics were, but I knew who the major players were at least. And not a single one seemed to have inherited an ounce of good luck.

\*\*\*

After a roast pork sandwich and a glass of sweet tea, I was going back to my computer when the phone rang. My father rushed into the kitchen waving his hand in the air.

"Let Asta answer it," he said, breathlessly. "I'm finishing the assistant module and want to see if I've got it right."

I sat down at the kitchen table and waited. He pressed a button on the wall mounted speaker box. "This is the Buchanan residence. Who's calling, please?" I laughed because my French-Canadian-born father had perfected the electronic equivalent of Queen Elizabeth.

"This is Sue Ellen Pruett, Margie Donovan's mother. I wanted to speak with AJ, please."

I was about to dash across the kitchen when I encountered my father's hand again. "Wait, you can take the call in a second," he whispered.

My mechanized assistant said, "Just a moment, please." Then the house was filled with a summons. "AJ, there is a call for you."

I grimaced at my father, then grabbed the portable phone off the cradle on the counter. "Mrs. Pruett, this is AJ. How are you? Is everything all right?"

I listened to her assurances that everyone was quite well, and I answered her questions about my new 'assistant'. My father grimaced and I winked. I moved to the speaker and hit the button so he could hear the conversation.

"Margie and the kids are getting settled, then?" I asked, pouring another glass of tea for myself and Papa. "It must be great to have them together and safe again."

"They do seem to be doing pretty well, but Sam is having some difficulty sleeping, and he's acting out in school. I'm a little worried about him."

I took a deep breath. "They've all been through a lot, Sue Ellen. And the kids process that kind of stress differently than adults do. They could probably all use some counseling. Is Margie looking for someone to work with them?"

"That's why I'm calling. She tells me they'll get over it and every time I prod her in that direction, she gets very angry with me and threatens to leave and never come back. My daughter makes her own decisions and that's fine, but I don't want to lose my grandchildren, AJ."

I tried to collect my thoughts. "Margie probably thinks she can handle it all, but that's unlikely. Few women who come out of what she has, do it without professional help. I know a couple of specialists in family-related post traumatic stress disorder, maybe I can get some referrals for you. Want me to call Margie and see if I can nudge her in the right direction?"

Her relief was audible. "You've done so much already, but I would appreciate your help. I don't know what else to do."

I assured her I'd call Margie in a day or two, after I spoke with the professionals I had in mind, and we ended the call.

My father looked as though he had something on his mind. "What is it, Papa?"

He tapped his bearded chin with the tip of his index finger. "This Margie, you think she really loves her children, yes?"

"Sure I do. Why?"

"A mother who loves her children would not want them to suffer with all the trauma. She would rush to get them help."

I nodded. "Under normal circumstances, of course. But she's been trying to keep everything together for so long, she may not know how to let go and trust someone to help them."

He shrugged and pushed away from the table, getting to his feet. "Or she may be frightened of them getting better."

"What? Why wouldn't she want them to get well?"

"Maybe what they have to say is different from what she told everyone."

"I guess that's possible, too. But it's more likely nothing that sinister. Not every rescued abused spouse or addict wants to do all it takes to live a normal life."

"And not every abused spouse kills her husband."

"There's that, too," I said, wondering why I was getting a bad feeling about Margie Donovan.

Had I helped a killer go free?

And how would Travis handle that, if that's what we'd done? He'd left law enforcement to prevent letting the bad guys go free. He knew firsthand how the innocent pay for that type of mistake.

***

Papa wanted to work on dinner, so I closed the door to my office and began to make those phone calls to my associates in the psychotherapy field. Two were unavailable, but "Doc" Carrie Siegel was delighted to speak to me.

"And how are you, Antonia? Catch me up! I haven't heard from you since you packed in the beltway."

I had to laugh. "That's only six years ago, Doc. I'm doing fine. I married a cop-turned-lawyer about a year and a half ago. It's working out fine."

"Is it hard work to keep it real or do you really mean it's working out well?"

"Some days are more of a struggle than others. I wonder why I married again if I wasn't ready, you know? But this guy is terrific, and he understands about Rick. He tries hard not to push me."

"So, if he leaves you alone, you agree to be happy, is that it?"

"I am happy, Doc. He loves me and I love him, too. Sometimes the ghosts show up, that's all. We both have some baggage, you know?"

"Oh, I know. As long as you remember that and respect that, love can survive. But you didn't call to talk about you, I'm sure. You didn't want to talk about yourself when the FBI *forced* you to see me."

I could hear the smile in her voice. Her quick intuition complimented her genuine concern for her clients, and I respected that. In another arena, we'd have been friends.

"You're right. Let me run something by you and see what you think is a sound recommendation for this family."

I told her the Margie Donavan story in abbreviated form, expanding only when she asked a direct question. I ended with Sue Ellen's request for help and my promise to see what I could do.

Doc was quiet for a while. "How well do you know Margie?" she asked.

"I don't know her personally. I often do investigative work for Travis. I interviewed her, ran down witnesses, arranged depositions, things like that. Seemed pretty genuine."

"But you have a soft spot for battered women, AJ. You would champion them and ask questions later. But you also follow your instincts. You felt she was telling the truth, right?"

"Right."

"Well, sometimes you just have to go with that. We can't always be right, but we're not always wrong, either. Maybe she just doesn't trust anyone not to put her children through more pain." She hesitated. "Therapy would only be effective if the children were made to face what transpired, you know."

I sighed. "Could she be afraid that the children remember things differently?"

Silence. "She could. But you know yourself, that ten eyewitnesses will all report seeing something different. That's why your photographic work was so important to the Bureau. Photographs don't lie." She laughed. "Or misinterpret."

"I can't push her, but I thought I'd call and check on her, see if she'll agree to going for some help. Will that make things impossible?"

I could picture Carrie's shrug. "It might but doing nothing when your instincts are telling you something is wrong, is worse. Go ahead and tell her to call me if you'd like. I have a friend with a PTSD practice that's in her area of the state. See what Mrs. Donovan says."

"Thanks, Doc. I appreciate it. You take care of yourself, okay?"

"I will. You do the same, AJ. Don't wait another six years to call me, okay?"

I agreed and hung up. Before I lost my nerve, I had a really hard call to place.

Before I could look up her number, my father tapped on the door.

"Someone here to see you, Antonia," he said quietly. He swung the door open, and I was glad I was sitting. The man standing behind him was surprised to see my sling but recovered fast. Then again, he always did.

"Hello, AJ. You wouldn't take my calls, so I decided to come to the mountain."

"Hello, yourself. There was a reason I didn't return your calls, you know. But since you're here, you might as well stay for dinner." I sounded a whole lot calmer than I actually felt.

"We really do need to talk, Darlin'. I'm catching the red-eye back to DC in a few hours."

A third man crowded the doorway and I smiled, knowing he'd startle my uninvited guest.

"What do you want with my wife, Mr. Flynn?"

# CHAPTER TWENTY-ONE

My office isn't quite big enough for me *and* two men well over six feet tall with egos to match.

I was beginning to suffocate with all that testosterone jetting around just as my father announced that dinner was ready. I didn't think I'd be able to swallow anything I put into my mouth, but we adjourned to the dining room, anyway.

The Cajuns are quite a cultured group of people. My father, with his dual Canadian and American citizenship, is still a Cajun, first. As hale and hardy and down to earth as they are, no matter who you are, all hostilities cease at eating time.

Travis sat beside me instead of his customary location on the opposite side of the table, leaving Joe Flynn to sit directly across the table from us both. No one spoke as my father passed around each plate of food so that we could serve ourselves.

Knives and forks clanked against the plates as we ate to avoid the inevitable conversation. When my plate was about half cleared, I put down my fork. My appetite was gone. Another bite and the whole meal would be coming back up.

"I can't believe that you came all the way to Nowhere, USA to talk to me, Joe."

"Antonia, this talk is going to be about death and other unpleasant things. Can't it wait until after dinner?"

I looked at my father and noticed that his eyes were ringed with dark circles. The scares and worries of the past three weeks had visibly aged him. I was sorry about that...I couldn't give him the time back and I knew our time together was getting shorter.

"Of course, Papa." Since I still couldn't reach out with my left arm, I asked for the cornbread. Travis held the basket so I could swipe the big piece with the butter melted on the top.

"You folks sure know how to eat down here," Flynn muttered, diving into his second helping of smashed potatoes.

"We know how to do a great many things, here," Papa said mildly. "The people in Washington D.C. forget that."

"The working people don't. And the politicians don't bother thinking about anyone at all, so it's not personal."

"How long have you made Washington your home?" Papa asked, pouring more sweet tea.

"Been there since I graduated Georgetown. That was almost forty years ago." He cleared his throat. "It's getting on time to move on, though. I just need to finish up a few things and then I'm turning over the reins to a new regime."

I sat back in my chair and looked at him. I remembered when I first met the crusty, order-barking news manager at the Washington Post. I was twenty-four and he was forty. He scared me so badly I shook and almost dropped my camera. And that was a year before I joined the FBI. Fourteen years later, I wasn't so easily intimidated. Or, Joe Flynn just wasn't the boogeyman that he once had been.

"You're looking at me like I've got something on my shirt," Flynn said, glancing down at his Bulldog's sweatshirt.

"Let's clean up and get you ready to catch that return flight, Joe," I said.

Travis removed the plate from my hand when I stood. "You and Flynn go ahead. I'll help your father with this."

He kissed my forehead and shot Flynn a look, then turned on his heel and followed my father out of the dining room and into the kitchen.

Joe followed me back to my office and made himself comfortable on the loveseat. I hid behind my desk in my high-backed chair.

"Why didn't you call me back, AJ? At least once? I didn't do anything to you that you'd have to hide from me. And what happened to Buchanan's face? And your arm?"

"We've been really busy here, Flynn. Travis was in a fire two weeks ago, and I was shot last week. We're sort of involved in a murder investigation and just finished a major court case. And I didn't call you back because you only call to nag me about coming back to DC to work on your conspiracy theory. I'm just not sure I can do that."

"I'm sorry about all the trouble you've had, AJ. If your father had told me, I'd have waited a little longer. But I can't wait too long."

I swung my booted feet up onto my desk and laced my fingers over my stomach, which was beginning to churn. I hoped he wasn't going to tell me what I feared most.

"I've got cancer, kiddo. Going to start radiation treatment in a few weeks, then maybe I'll have surgery, but of all my regrets, *you* are the only regret strong enough to keep me from hightailing it out of the city."

I nodded, very glad that Travis was in the kitchen. "I'm sorry you're sick, Joe. I noticed you didn't have cigarettes in your pocket. Is it lung cancer?"

"Nope, colon. But I gave up the cigarettes anyway, just to prove that I could." He smiled at me, his green eyes twinkling. "You know you're the one who got away, don't you?"

I laughed so hard I had to put my feet back on the floor. My rib and shoulder ached. "I know I was just one of many who got their big 'Joe Flynn' break by sleeping with you. Never had any illusions that it was serious, Joe. You treated me good, and I don't have any regrets about my time at the paper."

"Except one."

I shrugged. "Water under the bridge as the wise people say. Rick was killed in the line of duty. Sad as hell but happens all the time. We couldn't prove Hank Mangano killed him then, we can't prove it now. I've moved on. You need to do the same."

"Where's the woman that would face down an angry, gun-toting husband to save a battered woman? Where's the lady who'd spend her entire paycheck feeding the kids in the alley behind her apartment who lived in the cardboard boxes?"

I was too tired to trip down memory lane, so I waved off his guilt trip with my good arm. "Do you have new information that will help us get Hank or is this just something you need to do because you think you might die and leave it unfinished?"

He shook his balding head. "This needs to be done. Remember doing things because they needed doing, AJ? My sources say that Mangano is next in line for the assistant director position at the DEA. He's getting that nod at the expense of good officers who either died or left the agency because of him. He's probably the worst candidate for that job."

"So, tell the bureau chief. You're well respected in that town, Joe. You can be a royal pain in the ass, but they trust what you say."

"He wants proof. I can't get anyone to come forward and stand up to this guy."

Travis tapped on the door and then opened it, handing me a mug of steaming coffee. From the doorway, he faced Flynn. "So grown men are so terrified of this guy they won't fight for their jobs or justice, but you expect Antonia to do it?"

Flynn got to his feet, looking every bit of his sixty years. "I don't *expect* her to do it. I was hoping there was enough passion left in her that she'd agree to help."

"She'd agree in a heartbeat if you had something solid to go on. Without that, there's no reason for her to go back there and wallow in the past," Travis said quietly.

"You know yourself Travis, there's no forgetting when an injustice that size is committed," Joe started, shoving his meaty hands into the pockets of his khakis.

"You changed your entire life when that killer was set free to murder your witness. I'll bet you're still living with the face of that little girl in your dreams, just like AJ sees Rick being shot to death."

I slammed the coffee on my desk, the contents spilling all over the papers I had scattered on the blotter. "Not fair, Flynn. You have no right to pass judgment on me or Travis just because we've moved on. Everyone has to cope the best way they can when life dishes up shit. You always sat in your insulated office waiting for the dirt from the street to cross your desk. What the hell do you know about losing someone who's important to you?"

He moved toward the door, as red-faced and furious as I'd ever seen him. When he turned back to face us, I'd have sworn he'd aged another ten years.

"You're probably about the most important person I've ever had in my life. And I lost you twice." He winked. "Take care of yourself, kid. I'll see you around."

Travis and I stared at each other in utter amazement.

"Well, I'll be damned," said Travis.

"Me too," I whispered.

\*\*\*

"You're going back to D.C., aren't you?" my father asked.

Shaking my head, I sipped at the Jack Daniels in my glass. "Travis makes a good point. There is nothing I can do unless Flynn's got something concrete for us to work with. He doesn't. And people are going to speak to Flynn before they'll talk to me."

Travis remained uncharacteristically quiet. I knew that Flynn's jab was like a knife wound to my husband's soul. And, in traditional newspaperman style, Flynn had done his homework. The little girl Travis had sworn to protect was murdered by a man that had beat the judicial system.

Before the ink on the guilty verdict was dry, a technicality had let the brutal rapist go free so he could murder his victim. He eventually died in prison, but that brought no one any sense of relief. Her parents had spit in his face at her funeral, and Travis took a leave of absence from the police force.

He couldn't change the facts or bring that little girl back, but after the death of his parents, he decided to trade being a cop for being an attorney so that maybe, just maybe, he could get people the justice they deserved. But some nights he still battled the nightmares. Tonight, would probably be one of them.

"We've still got a lot of unfinished business here, right?" I said to the two of them. Father nodded. Travis stared into the fire.

"How sure are you that this Mangano guy was after Rick?" he finally asked.

"Everything I know would be considered circumstantial at best. Bits and pieces. Impressions. Rick and I were supposed to spend a weekend in the cabin we owned in North Carolina, but he was killed Thursday of that week. I went through the house, the cabin, the safe deposit box, and his locker at the gym so many times I lost count. I didn't find anything that had anything to do with Hank. But I know without a doubt, Rick was scared. And I know he was scared just as much for me as he was for himself."

"I know we've talked a little about this before, but apparently not enough. Why does Flynn think this guy is involved?"

"After Rick was killed, another agent went to Flynn and told him Hank had an off-shore account where a ton of drug money was stashed. He said he and Rick were working to prove that the account belonged to Mangano when Rick was killed."

Travis got to his feet. "That's enough for an indictment, AJ. Where's this agent now?"

"Arlington National Cemetery."

## CHAPTER TWENTY-TWO

"When did he die and how?" Travis sat on the edge of the couch, poised like a Jack Russell terrier on caffeine.

"Five years ago. Agent Farrell was killed in a hit and run accident. When neither Flynn nor I could find any hard evidence that the accident was a murder, I decided to stop chasing the ghosts and come back here. You know the rest."

"You still aren't going to tell me the whole story, are you?" he asked.

I looked at him a long time. He knew how much this still hurt me and he seldom pushed me about it, but maybe it was past time to get it out on the table.

"That's the Cliff Notes version, Travis. The details aren't important anymore. He and the team moved in for what was supposed to be a "routine" bust of some

223

interstate drug dealers and then before my eyes, it looked–and sounded–like the OK Corral.

"Anyway, I stayed in D.C. a full year after Rick's death using every connection and tool I had left at the Bureau to find out what really happened. We interviewed every member of Rick's team. Then Farrell showed up at Flynn's office one night, implicated Hank, and arranged to meet us when he got back from his assignment."

"And he never made it back."

I nodded. "He never showed up and we found out the following week that he'd been killed in North Carolina. Flynn, me, and a couple of friends sniffed around another few months. Nothing surfaced."

"And my daughter came home a walking dead woman." Father got to his feet and walked to the fireplace. "She was thin, no spark in her, only pain. With an old, dented camera."

I didn't even remember coming home, to be honest. I shrugged off the guilt. "Once I quit the FBI, it didn't make any sense to stay so close to the memories."

"I'm not sure going there again can bring you anything good, now."

"I know, Papa. For now, at least, I'm not going back. Let's just wait and see what happens with Flynn's surgery."

My father shook his head. "While the police are looking for Matilda's killer, you two could take a vacation, get better, enjoy living."

Travis laughed. "Nice idea, Henri, but I already tried that tact. Besides, we have an arsonist to find, a shooter to nail, a decorated veteran to bury and you know your daughter." He bowed and swept his arm in my direction. "Right, my dear?"

I swatted at him with my free hand. "Let's not forget about my father, the 'mad professor'."

My father smiled at me. "The attorney will help me with the insurance company if necessary. You should go away. Mend, rest." Then his eyes lit up. "And, before I forget again, I received an interesting call earlier today. A very large security firm from Sweden wants to discuss buying my system."

"Papa, that's terrific news. But how did a Swedish company know about ASTA?" I asked.

"I published a paper on it once the patent was filed. They claim they saw it in Computer World and American Inventors. I'm doing some checking on them before we speak again. I would rather it go to an American or Canadian firm, but in this global world, perhaps I'm being too naïve."

I couldn't wipe the grin off my face. "I'm proud of you. Just don't go signing anything until you've had an expert review it for you, okay?"

He got to his feet and placed his hand gently on my good shoulder. "I'm not senile yet, Antonia. And on that note, I think we should all get some sleep."

"Can the university terminate him early because of the explosion?" I asked Travis, standing to take my cup into the kitchen. The men followed me.

"I suspect they won't," Travis said. "He was working to support a greener, kinder planet and that's a cause that is in-vogue again now. His attorney is very press savvy, and I don't think the university will want the negative publicity."

"What a person does in their own home should not be punishable by law," Papa muttered, rinsing the mugs.

"If you don't blow up the neighborhood, it usually isn't," I said.

"Well, we'll just see what comes of all this. As I said, in May I am taking retirement anyway. I may decide to make an issue of academia and corporate American's reluctance to pursue natural alternatives to chemical pesticides and fertilizers."

"You are far too old for such idealism, Papa," I said, "but I do love you for it."

Travis put his arm around my shoulder and turned me toward the doorway. "Runs in the family, I guess."

"Did we get everything set for Sarge's funeral service?" I asked.

He followed me up the stairs to the bedroom. "What's this 'we' stuff? But yes, it starts at eleven. Better get a good night's sleep, Trouble. No telling what tomorrow will bring."

\*\*\*

Tuesday morning dawned damp and gray. Shane Davis called at nine-thirty to make sure we knew how to get to the Palatka Memorial Gardens. Since Travis had helped the Missing in America group to inter several unclaimed veteran's remains in that same cemetery, we knew it well.

When we arrived at the cemetery, a US flag-draped casket sat on a trolley, flanked by four Army honor guard in their dress blues. A dozen flag-bearing, Patriot Guard motorcycle riders stood at attention a short distance from the honor guard. Travis and I stood on the roadway by the car.

The young soldiers stood at attention, white gloved hands clutching their ceremonial rifles, shoes polished to a mirrored shine. The sky struggled to brighten our small, somber gathering.

Shane Davis arrived in his SUV, got out, and headed toward us, wearing his Putnam County Sheriff's Department uniform. Three men followed him, and I recognized the tallest of them from the day Betty and I had canvassed Palatka for information on our homeless stranger.

They were freshly shaved and sported clean pants and shirts, though tired sneakers peaked from beneath slightly tattered pant cuffs.

"Travis, AJ," he started, "want to introduce you to some of Sarge's friends." He shook our hands, then nodded at his guests.

"Nice to meet you," said the short, stocky man. "I'm Canton."

"I'm John," said the thin man that I recognized from the Methodist kitchen. At around six foot three, he couldn't have weighed a hundred seventy-five pounds.

"My name's Jeremiah," said the third man. We shook hands and stood in silence for a few minutes. Jeremiah's blue eyes were red-rimmed, his gray curls freshly cut.

"I talked to two men a few weeks back, George and James. Do they know about Sarge?"

John nodded. "They know. They scared. We ain't seen them in days."

"What's got them scared?" I asked. *Was Matilda's death tied up with the homeless situation, somehow?*

"You live on the street, you scared, that's all," said Canton.

"I supposed that's the truth." Made perfect sense to me. I lived in a house and was scared sometimes.

From the unmarked white van parked alongside the curb, a fifth man in dress uniform stepped out and walked toward us.

"That's the chaplain," said Shane. "They're real keen on showing this soldier the respect he deserves. Even on short notice."

Like a slightly mismatched family we began to walk the short distance to the gravesite.

"Sarge could be crazy, but he was a good man," Canton said. "Too bad he couldn't get respect *before* he died. He gave me his jacket one time, I was cold. Said he'd get another one. Give me food sometimes, too."

John looked at the open grave, his jaw tight, hands clenched. "He didn't deserve to die on them tracks. He wouldn't done that, Sarge. We was friends." His white hair fell forward on his forehead as he swiped his hand across his eyes.

"He was tired, John. Seen too much suffering. He couldn't keep on, that's all," said Jeremiah.

"Still don't believe it, that's all."

Jeremiah patted his friend on the back and Shane shook his head. "We don't have all the answers yet, so let's not jump to conclusions."

The Chaplain, a man who would have been an infant during the Gulf War, cleared his throat and we turned to give him our attention.

"We're here today to say thank you and goodbye to a good man. A husband, a father, a friend to many, and a soldier. Staff Sergeant Earl MacClellan served his country with pride and compassion."

He spoke without notes for almost ten minutes, in tones strong and clear. I stood to the side of the others so I could watch the area, but we were the only living souls in the cemetery. I stepped close to Travis when the honor guard raised their rifles to fire their final salute to the Sergeant.

Jeremiah, John, and Canton jumped in unison as the guns fired into the overcast morning. The report lingered in the air, even as the second shot was fired. When the gun salute was completed, one soldier handed his rifle to another, stepped back toward the Chaplain, saluted sharply, snapped his heels, and picked up his bugle.

As the last note of Taps hung in the air not one of us was dry-eyed. The soldiers folded Earl MacClellan's flag with great care, sharply creasing each fold, gloved hands smartly aligning the seams of each stripe. When the folding was completed to a perfect triangle, it was handed to the Chaplain.

He handed it to Shane Davis and saluted each of Sarge's friends. With a last salute to the Sergeant, the Captain led the honor guard across the wet grass, along the gravel walkway where they packed their blouses, guns, and bugle into the van.

We stood in comfortable silence as they drove away.

Shane ran a hand over the flag he held. "Sarge spent more time at the Methodist kitchen than anywhere else in town. They're going to hang his flag there. Since he doesn't have any family, seemed the right thing to do."

Jeremiah sniffed and nodded. "We can keep him close that way."

John reached into his back pocket and pulled out a small flip top pad. "Found this in a pocket of that coat he gave us. Do you want it, maybe? I was going to keep it, but then I got to thinking, maybe this will help you find who killed Sarge. Or that lady?"

He placed the book in my left hand, and I opened it with my right. Each page held an intricate, miniature pencil sketch. The Palatka waterfront with the new fountains; a sailboat in the cove; the Veteran's bridge with all the flags flying; a long-legged heron enjoying a just-caught fish. Travis and Shane looked over my shoulder.

I almost dropped it when I flipped a page and saw the mill. Vine covered, broken windows and all, he'd captured the dejected air of the abandoned building in his drawing.

"The man was incredibly talented," whispered Travis. I turned another page.

"Oh Lord," said Shane who was looking over my other shoulder. "Is that Matilda Renkin?"

## CHAPTER TWENTY-THREE

Canton and John stood beside Jeremiah who clutched Sarge's flag in his arms.

"Is that the lady you was looking for?" John asked.

"I'm not sure but could be. Thank you for giving this to us," I said. "When he can, Deputy Davis will get it back to you."

"Let's go to the diner and have some lunch," Shane said. "If you have time after that," he continued, nodding at me and Travis, "I'd like you to come to the office. Something you need to see."

We followed him to St. John's Avenue and parked in front of the storefront eatery. Our quiet gathering settled at a large round table in the back, away from the front windows.

"You know, Sarge would be proud of what we done today," Jeremiah said to Canton. The stocky man almost smiled, the first I'd seen.

"I just hope he's at peace. Man ain't had no peace in a long time," Canton said, slicing into the gravy-soaked meatloaf with his fork. "Fightin' wars to make peace just makes no sense, but Sarge never complained about that. He would cry sometimes, though. Know he seen some bad stuff."

John sighed. "I served as a medic, one tour. Spent sixteen months on a chopper, trying to get our boys out of the jungle." He tapped his empty right shirt sleeve. "Lost this on the last run out of Saigon. United Nations said we were done, get everyone out. Sniper fire got me and two others but didn't take down the bird. No matter how bad things got, I always been glad I made it home."

"I never left US soil. I put those boys on the planes at Fort Dix, New Jersey for close to ten years. Decided that was enough," Jeremiah said.

"Don't matter our skin color ain't the same. We all brothers 'cause we're veterans. We got nobody but each other and that's good enough," said John.

"Well, I've got a small law office up the street. I'd be proud to help you file for your veteran's benefits if you find you need help. No charge," Travis said. "And I need someone to take care of the building and grounds, most months. Anyone interested, stop and see me." He gave each man his business card.

Jeremiah reached across the table and shook our hands. "We'll do that, sir." He looked at me and smiled. "Your wife knows where to find us, if you need us before we show up."

***

We pulled into the parking lot behind Shane at the Putnam County Sheriff's office and then followed him through the doors. He signed us in, and we all traipsed into a small conference room.

"Be right back. I need to get my files."

Travis and I settled into padded folding chairs at a table, and waited, listening to the clock on the wall tick away the seconds. *Like Chinese water torture,* I thought. My collarbone and shoulder ached without the sling for support, and I rubbed them gently.

Shane pushed through the door with files under one arm and three bottles of water under the other.

"Thanks for coming. I wanted you to see the coroner's report which will get filed tomorrow. The press will have it before noon."

He spread the file open between Travis and me. "Sarge was already dead when the train ran him over..." Travis said. He looked at me. "You called it, AJ."

Shane rubbed the back of his neck. "That's what the doc found. We won't have tox back for a while, though.

But medical examiner says the BFT to the back of his head is probably what killed him."

"Blunt force trauma could have occurred upon impact by the train, couldn't it?" I asked.

"You're the forensic photographer. Look at these and tell me what you think."

I spread the high-quality digital photos out on the table. The scene was horrific, but the blood loss wasn't sufficient for death by impact. And his head and feet were untouched by the train impact.

"Going by these, I'd agree with your coroner. So, if the woman in Sarge's sketch book is Matilda, then we'd better proceed as though his murder is related to hers."

"That's how I'm thinking, too," Shane said, straightening the files and piling them on the table. He uncapped his bottle of water and took a long swallow. "I just wish I knew how you got dragged into this, and the poet definitely ties you into this."

Travis looked at me and then at Shane. "Whoever the killer is, thinks AJ has information she shouldn't have. We just don't know what it is."

"Maybe it's the diary?" I volunteered.

"But the threats came before you ever found the diary," Travis pointed out. "And let's face it. Where it was hidden, it might have stayed in that house a hundred years."

"You're right. But the poems definitely make this about the Renkin family."

Shane tapped his fingers on the table. "We got a call from Clay County last night. They picked up Bobby Joe Fletcher."

"Well, that's good news. I'd just love ten minutes with that son of a bitch," said Travis.

"We have a little problem with him as the shooter. Seems he reported his truck stolen a day before Margie Donovan was set free."

"Stolen? That couldn't be too hard for a good old boy to arrange, could it?" Travis was pacing in a four-by-four foot pattern. He was hard to rile, but when he got going, he was even harder to calm down.

"Claims he got so drunk he passed out, came to and he was on his front porch, no truck, no keys, no idea how he got there. Reported his truck stolen that afternoon."

"So what," I asked, "someone else took a shot at Margie?"

"According to the Gainesville Police Department, he borrowed his mama's car for the rest of that week so he could get to and from work. We're still checking out some facts, like was he even at the courthouse that day. We know he wasn't at work, but since the truck's still missing, we're going to have to get resourceful to nail him on evidence."

"I'd like to be here when you talk to him. Can you arrange that?" Travis asked.

Shane shook his head. "He's got no alibi for the fire. We're looking hard at him for that, too. The whole thing will be taped, so you can review those. Chief would prefer you weren't in attendance, though."

Travis grunted.

I stood beside him. "Any more information on the detective that picked Richard up and dropped him off here in Palatka for the car?"

"No and we've exhausted the active-duty roster. My boss has coordinated our retiree roster with the U.S. Marshal's office. They'll have Richard go through those photos tomorrow. We're getting no hits on a Lieutenant Barnes."

"Maybe he got the name wrong. Or, maybe the agency. Might not be Putnam County Sheriff's Office. If Dora was involved in the arrangements to get Junior from the airport to Palatka, she should know how to reach her friend, right?" I asked.

"She's a strange lady, that one. She had no idea what anyone was talking about. The deputy that spoke with her said she seemed very confused. She couldn't get anything useful from her."

Travis nodded. "We had a conversation with her that was odd, too. I wonder if she's on medication of some sort? Or should be?"

Shane shrugged. "No idea and we can't really ask. Let's see if Junior can come up with anything to help us out. If not, maybe we can get some information from her friends at the church. Seems to be her only other social network."

Travis and I stood and shook hands with Shane. "We'll wait to hear from you about Fletcher. You need us before then, just call."

\*\*\*

We'd just reached the base of the Palatka Veteran's bridge when my cell phone buzzed. I glanced at the display. Margie Donovan was calling.

I plugged it into the hands-free unit on the dash of Travis's truck so he could hear the conversation as well.

"Hi, Margie. How are you?"

"We're all fine, AJ. Can you take me off speaker, please?" she asked.

"I'm with Travis, no one else. Do you mind if he hears our conversation?"

"No, that's fine, I guess. You both helped me and my kids out a lot. I hope you know how much I appreciate all you did for us."

Travis looked at me. "We do, Margie. We were glad to help," he said.

She sighed. "You need to stop poking around now, though. I don't need doctors I can't afford and my kids don't need them either. I know my mother called you and she had no right. We don't need anybody interfering anymore. I know you mean well, but I'll run my own life."

"Your mother's worried about you with all you've been through, that's all. And frankly Margie, the court is going to insist that the children get counseling. It's part of the terms of probation, you know that. The doctors I suggested to your mother won't cost you anything and they are some of the best in the business."

The line was silent, but the display showed the call was still connected. "We aren't your concern anymore. Do you understand me? Stay out of my life."

"What are you afraid of Margie? Anything discussed between you and your doctors can't be shared with anyone else. And besides, you're protected by the Law of Double Jeopardy," Travis said. "You can't be tried again for the murder of your husband, even though a jury never decided your case."

"You sound as though you think I am guilty, Travis," she said softly.

I answered her, my hands clasped so tightly in my lap they were white-knuckled.

"Something your mother said when she called me. You give the kids a homeopathic sleep medication at dinner time, according to your mother. But the kids hadn't been medicated the night you shot your husband. Since you were having dinner before he came home, I had to wonder why you broke your routine that night. Add in the fact that you don't want the kids to get counseling, makes me wonder about all those little discrepancies."

"Doesn't matter now really, does it? He was a mean, hurtful man and I wasn't going to be hurt any more. Wasn't going to risk him hurting my babies."

"And bullets cost a lot less than divorce."

Her silence echoed in the truck. "Divorce wouldn't mean he couldn't still kill me, take my kids. I risked going to jail until my children were full grown, but at least I knew they would be safe. You don't have kids, you don't understand."

Travis reached across the seat and placed his hand over mine. "I understand better than you think."

*He sure as hell does.*

"I had to do what I could to be here for my children."

He took a deep breath and then let it out. "I'm damned disappointed that you lied to me. But I think I understand why you did what you did."

He made the turn onto Sycamore Street. "If you violate your parole, any aspect of it, the State of Florida will prosecute you to the fullest extent of the law. I won't be available for counsel a second time."

"Thank you, Travis," she said.

I shook my head, but I understood too. I wasn't convinced that she was wrong, even knowing the truth. Wonder what that made me. A vigilante-in-training, maybe? *Lord have mercy on us all.*

"Take care, Margie Donovan," I said before ending the call. "And Happy Thanksgiving."

## CHAPTER TWENTY-FOUR

When I woke Thanksgiving morning, the smells of sautéed celery and onions mingled with brewed coffee. The bedside clock said six-forty-five and Travis still slept soundly beside me.

I eased out of bed careful not to lean on my shoulder, searched the floor with my bare feet for my flip flops, and headed downstairs to the kitchen.

"Good morning, Papa." I reached for the coffee pot.

He looked up from the island counter where cubed bread and a sea of spice jars littered the cutting board.

"You are up too early. Go back to bed and rest, Antonia."

"I'm fine, Papa. I can stir and chop, even if I can't wrangle the turkey and mash the turnips."

"Everything is done except for the stuffing. Mrs. Macomber and I roasted pecans yesterday. When this is done, I'll stuff the bird and into the oven he goes. Not much else to do except heat everything up."

I sat at the table with my coffee. "You invited Mrs. Macomber to join us, yes?"

"Of course. She thought better of it though. Said it's too dangerous to eat here, no telling what will blow up or catch fire next. She asked us to come over for dessert."

"My neighbors don't have any sense of humor. A little fire and some gunshots and she's all worried. This is Florida for goodness sakes. Here those things are normal, everyday occurrences."

"Not in this town, Antonia. At any rate, I did not commit for you and Travis, but I'm going over this evening."

"Okay, Papa, let's just play it by ear. I'm going in my office and get some work done, before Travis gets up."

Before I could exit stage right, Papa stopped me. "Where are Betty and Michael today? This will be a very hard holiday for Betty. All the 'first' holidays without someone you love are hard."

"I know, Papa. I asked them to join us, but Michael's mother and brother's family live in Atlanta so they went there. He had some work come in, too. They won't be back until Sunday, she said."

"I don't know her Michael, but she seems happy?" he asked as he stuffed his aromatic concoction deep into the center of the luckless fowl.

"I don't know him either, but I'd say she really loves him. And if my instincts are any good at all, he's crazy about her, too. But there's something there—something that's bothering him. Has something to do with Richard."

Senior or Junior?" he asked

"Junior, I'm sure. Something Betty said when we were working at the house."

"His mother-in-law has been murdered. He and his wife needed alibis. That would unsettle anyone, wouldn't it?"

I sipped at my coffee. "I guess, but I think it started before Matilda was killed."

"You'll figure it out." Papa opened the oven door and slid the turkey inside. Then he pulled out the keyboard and typed something to Asta.

"You're trusting our Thanksgiving dinner to the computer?" I asked.

"She is your assistant, not just a computer. She will monitor the probe in the oven and made sure it is not overdone. I'm going back to bed. We don't have to be up this early."

With that, he marched himself out of the kitchen. I poured a fresh cup of coffee and moved into my office. Sleep sounded delightful, but once I'm awake, I'm awake.

I filed the paperwork that lay on my desk as I waited for my computer to boot up. I tucked the clipping of Sarge's death and the funeral notice, into the Mayfield file. I didn't know how his death was connected, but I knew it was.

Shortly after I settled into my chair and dove into my emails which now numbered over five hundred unanswered messages, I saw it.

"Happy Thanksgiving, Gothic Poet," I whispered to the empty room.

"Don't open that, Antonia," my father said from the doorway, nearly making me jump out of my skin. "Save it as a PDF to a flash drive. Then I think it may open without self-destructing."

The flash drive blinked as the file downloaded. "I thought you were going back to bed." My heart rate was still far too fast for holding a conversation.

"I did, but I couldn't go back to sleep. Let's see that poem."

I located the file on the directory and double clicked. It opened, looking like a scanned message out of an old mystery novel, with letters of various type styles and sizes pasted onto a piece of paper.

> *Another one dead, the count is now three,*
> *They are all dying since you won't listen to me.*
> *Let the secrets rest, or the price that you'll pay,*
> *will leave you grieving on His judgment day.*

244

"Secrets," I whispered.

"Well, you have uncovered quite a few of late. You need to call Deputy Davis."

"Not today, Papa. It's Thanksgiving and he actually has a couple of days off. This will keep until tomorrow at least, I'm sure." I looked back at the screen. "How did you know that the message could be saved this way?"

"It's an attachment. The last one had a viral signature that one of Asta's programs detected. But it needs to be opened in the initial location to activate the virus. Taking it out of there made the virus impotent."

"Speaking of secrets, what have you decided about Matilda's secrets?" he asked.

"When Betty gets back to town, I'm going to give her the diary and the rest of her mother's papers. She deserves to know the truth. That's what she asked of me when her mother died."

Travis appeared, sleepy-eyed, hair falling across his forehead. "That's going to mess her up. I hope she can handle it."

Was everyone in my family a blasted insomniac? "She's going to hurt like hell, but she's strong. And she's got Mike. She'll be okay." I typed a reply to my cyber-stalker.

"What are you doing, Antonia?" Papa asked.

I winked at him. "I'm done playing with this joker. The secrets are no longer secrets. Maybe we can either flush this guy out or make him go away."

Travis looked at me, his eyes narrowed. "Another love letter, I presume?"

Papa nodded. "I don't think taunting this person is smart, but then my daughter, the hot-shot-FBI-trained private investigator knows better than *everyone* else."

"Aren't you tired of this waiting for something else to happen? I don't want to play anymore. I want this over with." I hit the send key with a flourish.

My father sighed, a sound I knew well. "You should be careful about what you wish for."

## CHAPTER TWENTY-FIVE

Friday morning after our quiet Thanksgiving, Papa breezed into the kitchen.

"I'll be spending the day with Mrs. Macomber. We're going to play tourist in St. Augustine and have dinner at the Sea Fair. She says they have prime rib that is out of this world." He smiled. "I won't be back early. You two have plenty of leftovers for dinner."

Was my father getting serious about another woman? My mother had been dead for twenty years, so why did the idea pinch me?

"Make sure you thank her for our dessert plate," I said. "I can't wait to get into the sweet potato pie."

"You'll like that. It isn't as good as your mama's, but it is good." He poured a glass of water into the red Poinsettia plant on the counter.

I looked at Travis over the rim of my coffee cup and beneath a raised brow, he winked at me. I almost spit my coffee out.

"Have a good time, Papa," I choked.

"You don't need to get that look in your eye. You'll always be my best girl," he said, then kissed the top of my head. He pulled his jacket off the hook behind the door.

"We're going to Gainesville tomorrow so I can check on the house repairs. The contractor should be about done with the kitchen." With a wave he was gone, like a geriatric ninja.

"He didn't have any breakfast," I muttered.

"Maybe they're having breakfast together, who knows?"

"I wonder if he's serious about her? Would I have to call her 'Mom' if he marries her?"

Travis laughed. "Your father would expect you to be respectful, nothing else. She already mothers you anyway, so what's the difference?" He took our dishes to the counter. "I wonder if they'd live here or in Gainesville?"

"I wonder." The prospect of my father living across the street from us was not entirely distasteful. Would they get married or just lived together? I found the question bothersome and frowned.

Travis took me by the hand. "How about we take a ride and visit Silver Springs today? They've got the early Christmas concerts starting in the park. If you're up to it, maybe we'll ride a couple of the roller coasters, too."

"Are you suggesting that we take a day off and go play, Crimestopper?"

He pulled me into his arms and rested his chin on my head. "I am, indeed, Trouble. I think we've earned it, don't you?"

"I do. I'll go shower-you leave my father a message with Asta."

Spending a day in Silvers Springs made me feel as excited as a kid. I skipped up the stairs. Relaxing was just what the doctor had ordered. And everyone else, too.

\*\*\*

The phone rang at nine-thirty on Saturday morning but before I could roll over to answer it, the ringing stopped.

The blowing palm trees brushed stiffly against the windows, creating a sound like rattling shutters. The colorless morning looked bleak. I pulled on my blue flannel Gator pants and matching sweatshirt and headed down the stairs to the kitchen.

Papa smiled when he saw me and pulled a mug from the cupboard to pour me coffee. I nodded and slid into the pew.

"Did you have a good day yesterday, Papa?"

"We did. I'd forgotten how nice it is to have someone to do tourist things with. The Old City is so beautiful with the Nights of Lights celebration going on.

April Macomber is a lovely lady. Smart and funny. We took the horse carriage tour. I'm sure it wasn't entirely accurate, but it was very entertaining."

"That's great. I'm glad you've made friends while you're here. Do you have any idea how much work still has to be finished at your place?"

"I'm not sure. Harry's been going back and forth across the street to water the orchids and make sure the heater is working, but he said he hadn't been inside the house." He shrugged. "He says the workman's truck is there every day, though."

"Just be sure you're happy with all that's been done," I said. "Regardless of who ends up paying for the repairs, you have to be pleased."

I looked through the glass in the kitchen door at Travis who was out on the porch talking on his phone. He turned and saw me and put his index finger in the air to indicate that he'd be done in a minute. I smiled. Despite fires and gunshots, holidays and explosions, life continued on.

He came through the heavy oak door and closed it against the cool morning air. "Sleep well?" he asked.

"I did. My shoulder is killing me, though." I tried to lift my arm which almost made me cry. "Must have been that damned roller coaster ride yesterday. Heard the phone. Someone need representation?"

"Not exactly. Shane called to say he's got a line on Dora's Lieutenant."

"Terrific! Maybe now we can figure out what's going on with this whole thing. How'd they find him?"

"Davis kept running the name through the law enforcement databases and got a break. The guy's been retired for almost fifteen years from the Gainesville Police Department."

"So he wasn't at any seminar in Gainesville, right?"

"He was there all right. He still teaches FDLE classes. Forensic crime scene investigation techniques."

"That's very interesting. Well, we both know fire fighters have been known to start arson sprees, and nurses become well-intentioned grim reapers, so maybe our cop is a serial killer. Might even think he has justification for it. He has the knowledge to pull off the perfect crime, doesn't he? When will they talk with him?"

"Unknown. Davis doesn't want to spook him, so he's inviting him to the station as soon as possible. We can observe the interview tape. Said to figure sometime Monday, at the earliest."

"Good. Glad it won't be today. I feel like hell. You going into the office for a while?" I didn't need him fussing over me all day.

He nodded. "If you'll be okay here, I am. Weather's supposed to get nasty later this afternoon. Nor'easter, lots of wind and rain. But I have to be back to court on Monday and I don't have my files here."

"When's the contractor coming about the garage?"

"End of next week, or that's what he said. That'll give us time to decide what to do with your Corvette."

"You said you knew someone in Palatka that does restorations, right?"

"I'll stop by today while I'm over there and see if he's interested in doing it." He looked at me. "I'm sorry you're in so much pain. You going to be okay here by yourself?"

"You bet. Take your male selves out of here and I'll get Betty's papers together. She's coming over whenever they get back from Georgia. Monday, I think. I'll just take it nice and slow today."

"Get some rest, honey. And take something for the pain, don't suffer with it. Bad weather isn't helping, I'm sure."

"Right. I'm going to shower, then I'll be in the office." I looked at my father. "Please be careful driving to Gainesville."

He smiled. "I'll let you know if we're not coming back, but I suspect April's not put off by a little bad weather."

"No, just fires and gunshots," I mumbled under my breath.

"I heard that, young lady," Papa said. "Get some rest. You're grouchy."

My husband snagged his brief bag and jacket and ducked between me and Papa. "Love you," he called as he dragged my father out the door.

"Love you too," I said to the space where they'd been a second earlier.

By the time I'd eaten a fried egg sandwich, swallowed an oxycodone, and luxuriated in a hot shower, I felt decidedly better. The gray day hadn't brightened any. I lit the fireplace and left the door to my office open so I could look through the doorway and see the flames licking carelessly all around the gas logs.

The scraping of the tree limbs against the house sounded like fingernails on a slate wall and set my teeth on edge.

I opened my Skype program and called Flynn at the Post. I got his out-of-office message, so I called his home number.

"Flynn, here," he grumbled. He hadn't accepted the video portion of my call, but at least he was talking to me.

"Hey, Joe. How are you feeling?"

"I'm tired as hell, puking most of the time and wish this was over already. Not sure if this chemo shit is going to kill me or cure me. Other than that, I'm just fine."

"Since you are complaining like a bear with an infected paw, I'll take that as a good sign," I said. "You still on for the surgery?"

"Depends on what the next scan shows. They want to do that next week. If the radiation's shrunk the tumor enough for them to go in and clean it all out, I'll have surgery week after Christmas."

"Is someone going to stay with you?" I wished I hadn't asked. What the hell would I do if his answer was no?

He was silent. "I'm going to my sister Melissa's in Arlington. She wants me to stay there until I'm healed."

"I'm glad Joe. I wouldn't want you to be alone after a surgery like that."

"Would you have come to take care of me if I was?"

I laughed. "No, nursing wounded bears isn't my strength, but I know some great rehab facilities up there. Specialize in really tough cases."

"Bitch."

"You bet," I said. "I just wanted to check on you. Take care of yourself and let me know how you're doing, okay?"

He was silent. Then, "Do you really care, AJ?"

I smiled even though he couldn't see it. "Of course, I care. We've always been friends, no matter what else, right?"

"Sure," he sighed. "I'll keep in touch. Gotta go." Then the call disappeared from my screen, and he was gone.

I got up from my desk and stretched as much as I could given that the pain in my left shoulder almost dropped me to my knees.

I grabbed the copy paper box that I'd stashed Betty's papers in and moved into the living room. I laid everything out on the floor and sat on the couch with pad and pen to catalog it all.

The wind was howling. Every now and then the windows in our old house rattled and the lights flickered. I got up and lit the candles on the mantle just in case the wind took down the power lines, then instructed Asta to put on the satellite jazz station. Bonnie Raitt crooned through the house, almost harmonizing with the sounds of the storm.

I photographed, logged, and then slipped the single sheets of paper from the box into acid-free plastic evidence sleeves. I opened the diary and laid it on the coffee table, pages open wide. I decided against photographing it. If Betty wanted to burn it and pretend it never existed, I intended to honor that wish. I closed it, wiped the leather cover clean and placed it back in the box just as the phone rang.

"Hello?" I pressed the speaker button on the phone as the lights flickered and the house rattled. Travis's voice was crackling like lightening.

"AJ, honey, your father just called me. He's not going to make it back tonight. Gainesville's getting creamed by this storm. He said they've had more than four inches of rain since noon."

"Are they okay?"

"They're fine," he said. "But he's doing the best thing by staying there. We don't need any more calamities right now."

I laughed. "You're right. Are you going to be able to get home? I think we've got more wind with this storm than during the last two hurricanes."

"I know. I'm going to do my best," Travis said. "Florida Highway Patrol just closed Veteran's Bridge, though. I'm going to wait it out here and see if they reopen it in the next couple of hours. All law enforcement is out on the roads, but Shawn's going to check with me. If he can't get me back across the bridge, I'll drive around—"

At that moment, the lights went out, leaving me standing in the shadows of candle and firelight. "Travis?"

The phone was dead. Although I never had enough bars on my cell phone to call anyone from home, I picked it up and checked anyway. No signal.

"Asta?" I called out. I glanced at the control panel on the wall which was dark. The generator tie-in was scheduled for later in the week. *Timing is everything...*

"Damn," I muttered, wishing I had skipped the pain killer. Moving in slow motion, I crossed to my office, reached in the drawer, and got my .38, dragged myself into the living room and curled up on the sofa to wait for Travis's return. I pulled the afghan over me and let my heavy eyelids close.

A crash woke me. A cold wind blew through the room as I struggled to get to my feet without using my bad shoulder. I heard glass crunching under someone's feet as I shook my head to clear it. I couldn't seem to wake up.

The shadows of the candles and fire light danced on the wall. The power was still out.

Finally on my feet, I turned back to the table to get my gun. The crunching had stopped.

"Hand me your weapon, Mrs. Buchanan."

# CHAPTER TWENTY-SIX

For a millisecond I wondered what she was talking about, and why she was in my house, and what the hell was damaged now.

Since I was obviously not reacting quickly enough, she fired a shot past my left ear, splintering the window frame and shattering the glass. The drug fog in my brain was replaced by a loud ringing. I pressed my hands over my ears to clear them.

"I'm really tired of being shot at, Dora. How in the hell did you get into my house?"

"Through the kitchen door, of course. I'm sure you are aware that it is generally the home's weakest link in security. A good old fashioned tire iron is a marvelous tool for breaking windows and opening locked doors. Besides, I think that if you'd mind your own business, and that Casanova of a husband kept his hands to himself, people wouldn't be shooting at you. Sit down."

I sat. Not a problem. "You've met my husband once, a week ago. What would give you the idea he's a Casanova?"

"I saw him in the church, his hands all over Betty. I know his kind, using women and throwing them away like an empty coffee cup. And women like you who permit it."

I racked my brain. Had Travis touched Betty? When? "Travis is a good man, Miss Dora. He protects women from men who hurt them. Protecting people is his greatest passion."

She laughed but the gun never wavered. "They protect women to make them dependent. Dependent women are weak. Needy women have to rely on the men who take care of them. Natural victimology, you know."

I looked at my hands. "Who hurt you so badly, Dora?"

"The men in my life have been hurting me since my conception. Taking whatever suited them. My birthright, my name, my money, my daughter, my legitimacy."

"I don't understand." *Keep her talking...*

"Too bad. You don't need to understand."

I kept my voice as even as I could. "But I'd like to. Betty's my friend. Matilda was, too. Please tell me why you're so angry."

"You want to know? Well, why not. And you'll be the last one to hear the story. With me, and you, it's over."

"Okay," I said. *This is not sounding good....*

"My father was Joshua who was also Matilda's father. He and his sister Sarah were twins. He believed that she was the only one worthy of his love and he consummated that love with her. By rape or consent I do not know. Sarah, my mother, died when I was a few hours old, so my father's wife, a simpering woman named Anna, took me as her own. Anna died when I was eleven and she told me everything before she died. Silly woman thought she was protecting me or something."

She wasn't distracted, but if she was talking, she wasn't shooting. "Did Matilda know the truth about your mother?" I asked.

"I promised Father if he ever laid a hand on me again, I'd tell the whole world his dirty little secret. He obviously believed me because he turned his attentions to Matilda. She was far too unhappy to give me a thought once he found her an acceptable substitute. And he never showed up in my bedroom again."

She stared into the fire. "Matilda thought I was her full-blooded sister until Betty was born. I hadn't meant to tell her the truth then, but the birth was so difficult, and I was out of my head with pain. I must have spewed out everything. Mattie cried for the longest time, and I just prayed she'd go away, but she sent the midwife away and cared for me, promising me everything would be okay.

"Then Richard came and took the baby away. Said I was unfit to raise a child. Matilda swore until the day I ended her sorry life that she did not know he was going to take my baby away from me. But, even if she didn't, she was just like Anna. Looking out for their husbands in all their evil doings."

"You and Richard Senior were lovers," I said.

"We were soul mates, not just lovers. Or that's what I thought at the time. Richard should have been *my* husband, not Matilda's. He didn't love her, but Richard wanted my father's wealth and businesses and my father despised me for my rejection by that time." She smiled.

"Matilda couldn't stand Richard until she realized it was a way to escape my father. I adored Richard, but my father wouldn't hear of my marrying. He'd have put me away rather than allow me to be happy."

She was no longer focused on me, though I wasn't making any quick moves. She was nuttier than a Georgia pecan pie and I had no doubt she'd shoot me in a heartbeat.

"I'm Betty's friend, Dora. And I promise you Travis wouldn't hurt her, either. She's happily married to a good man; she isn't haunted by all this old history. Put the gun down, go home and this is over."

The gas-fed fire sputtered, the candles on the mantel cast long gold shadows on the wall. I inched closer to the edge of the sofa.

"Stay where you are, young lady," she said. "Your husband will not hurt Betty because I'm going to kill him, too. You would never let it rest and you know enough to hurt my Betty. I know your kind. You're all about telling the truth no matter who you hurt. You must die. It would seem that the only way to have anything done right is to do it myself."

"You're the poet, aren't you?"

"Of course. But you are so stubborn, you didn't listen."

"Why did you kill Matilda?" I asked.

Her eyes widened, her breath quickened. "She slept with my husband and helped Richard to steal my daughter. My happiness, my rightful place in the family has always been completely ignored. Then Matilda was going to fly to Arizona and turn her back on everything. Betty would have no one to protect her and Matilda promised never to leave my daughter behind. I've paid quite enough for Matilda's happiness."

I decided that reasoning with a deranged woman who held a loaded gun was foolish, even though I knew Matilda had very little happiness in her entire seventy-five years. Seemed a moot point. "What about the homeless man? And the fire?"

She shrugged, waving her free hand as though she was shooing a fly. "Senseless diversions, I'm afraid. Meant to scare you, but unfortunately, you don't scare easily. When you were shot, I was afraid that you'd die before I got all of Matilda's papers secured. You gave me quite a fright. It wouldn't do for those things to fall into the wrong hands, you know."

She glanced at the box on the floor by the bookcase and I wished that I hadn't used a bold-tipped black marker to put Matilda's name on all sides. Dora used the barrel of her .45 to motion me toward the fireplace.

"Why don't we start with these, while we wait for your husband to return?"

"He's stuck in Palatka because they closed the bridge. He may not get home until tomorrow."

"Not to worry about that. One thing at a time, dear," she muttered. "Start putting those papers in the fire. You didn't make copies of anything, did you?"

"Every page," I said.

"You're a liar, Mrs. Buchanan. Understandable I suppose, but not an attractive quality."

I ignored her. "Did you kill Sarge and set my garage on fire?"

"If you are referring to the transient who saw me with Matilda at the mill, his death, though regrettable, was quite necessary. My associate insisted that the vagrant be disposed of and managed that without my supervision. Turned out his idea about the fire wasn't as carefully expedited. I told him you would not be frightened off by a little fire."

"Would your friend be the retired Lieutenant Barnes that picked up Junior at the airport a few weeks ago?"

She smiled. "Very good. He used to be a reliable accomplice. Now he's more of a liability."

"Why in the world would he help you to hurt people?"

"He and I share many of the same values, one could say. When I was in nursing, I helped him kill his wife. He's helped me with various 'inconveniences' ever since."

"He murdered his wife?" I asked.

"I didn't say murder, did I? She was very sick and wanted to die but the doctors were doing all they could to keep her alive, in all the excruciating pain and agony that accompanies ovarian cancer."

"So you assisted in her suicide."

"Exactly. However, the sovereign state of Florida does not see it that way. That has been a good thing for me, actually. As I said, Barnes has been a valuable ally over the years."

I rubbed my pounding temples to clear my thoughts. "Why didn't you just kill Travis and me the day we visited you at your home?"

"One doesn't kill people in one's own home. It's in very poor taste. Besides, I still had hopes at that time you would just let this go. When the police showed up asking questions about my retired friend, I knew I'd have to clean it all up."

She waved the big gun at me again, though her eyes looked a bit more vacant. She either needed medication or had taken too much.

"Enough talking. Get those papers into the fire."

I picked up the medical papers which were on top of the diary, slowly slipped them out of the sleeves and laid them on the fire. They were so old and brittle, the flames flared for little more than a couple of seconds, and the documents were ash.

I favored my injured shoulder and reached into the box with my right hand. Maybe burning everything wasn't such a bad idea, but I still felt badly that Betty would never know the truth for herself.

I took the diary out of the box and laid it to the side. I'd do all I could to save it.

I fed newspaper articles and many of my own notes to the fire. Much of this information was on my computer. If I lived through the day, I had easy access to the information again. Even if Dora thought to ruin my computer, it was all secured in an online vault.

The genealogy I'd done to ascertain all of the players in the Mayfield-Renkin history went up in smoke with the rest of it, though it burned far more slowly and with less color. Paper was obviously not the quality product it had been back when the Mayfield's had run the paper mill.

Finally, I straightened from where I was crouched at the hearth and Dora stood as well. I rubbed my lower back and my shoulder. The old diary with *RICHARD RENKIN* in gold-leaf letters was all that remained. Dora stared at it.

"Open that book. Then move away."

I did as she asked. She motioned me into the corner, then stared at Richard's notations.

For a moment, the lights flickered on, startling us both. Asta began to shriek about the back door being breeched when the power went off again. At least Travis would see the broken window in the kitchen and be cautious coming in....

The light, brief though it was, had illuminated the face of a bitter old woman, madness her companion for far too long. Her grey eyes glittered, her chin trembled, and I hoped that the gun would lower, but it never wavered.

"He really was quite a cruel man, wasn't he?" she asked no one in particular. She turned a page and read on. "He threatened to snuff out Betty's life here, but he'd never do that to his own child. When Matilda told me how she killed Richard, I thought it fitting that she should die the same way. They both betrayed me, you know."

"I know, Dora."

"Betty is not like either of us, is she?"

"She's smart and kind and generous and brave. I always thought she was a lot like Matilda, actually. Now I know her a little better than I did when we were kids. She's her own person. As we told you during our visit, Betty went into nursing because of how much she admired you."

She looked at me for a long moment. "A medical career is the best way a woman can ensure she'll always be able to support herself. Mattie didn't want Betty to be dependent on any man. I was always happy about that. It's sad that Mattie never learned it for herself, though. She was a whore in return for security."

"Betty loves you, even if she doesn't know you are her mother. What you're doing tonight means Betty is going to lose you, too. She truly will have no one to protect her. She may not need anyone for her financial security, but family is really important. Maybe we can still work all this out."

She smiled at me like I was an imbecile. "I know that I am schizophrenic. Well, at least today, I do. Some days the medication works better than others." She laughed and shrugged. "The doctors have treated me for years. But the dementia will only get worse. The best thing I can do for Betty is to destroy the evidence of this awful deed and clean up the mess I've made of things. She'll be safe then. She'll get over the losses. Once always does."

I stared at her, speechless. She looked at me and winked like we were co-conspirators in some grand play.

"Yes, I know my mental faculties are not what they should be. Incest can have that affect on the unfortunate offspring."

Swallowing hard, I tried to reason with her. "If you realize that, you know that the legal system has provisions for mental defect. You don't have to kill me and Travis to save Betty."

"A trial would only shame her. After all I've told you, you don't understand at all. Perhaps you are not as bright as I thought. Everything I've done is to save her all the humiliation. You have no idea how damaging humiliation can be."

The lights flickered and the wind didn't rattle the windows like it had earlier. If the storm had abated, the bridge would reopen. *Travis is headed straight into an ambush.*

Dora was tiring. For more than an hour she'd held me at gunpoint. Anything was better than sitting around waiting for the bullet that would end my life. Or my husband's. I had to do something.

I made a mental note of Dora's position in the room. Ready to use the emergency switch to kill the fireplace, I stepped toward the wall. Dora didn't seem to notice. The candles had burned out a half hour ago.

The phone rang and the lights flashed again before darkness surrounded us again. Dora was startled, looking wide-eyed around the room as though she didn't know where she was or why she was there.

I killed the fire and dove for where Dora was seated on the settee with the journal. I couldn't see her, but heard the book hit the floor, which meant she'd moved.

Something hard cracked me in the head, and I obviously missed my target. I got to my feet and swung left, right into the barrel of the Colt.

We wrestled for it in the dark, my ribs shooting knife-like pain through my body while my shoulder felt like it was being ripped from the socket.

"Dora, stop right now," a deep male voice commanded. "It's over."

I heard her laugh as I fought to catch my breath, my head reeling and the pain in my ribs and shoulder so bad I thought I'd pass out. Blood ran into my eyes.

"Who's going to stop me? You?" she screeched.

Two muzzles flashed and shots rang out. A roar filled my head as I collapsed on the hearth rug.

The last thought I had was that once again, I'd failed to stop the death of the man I loved.

# CHAPTER TWENTY-SEVEN

When I came to, the lights were on, and I was lying on the floor looking at shoes. Several pairs of shoes. Lots of talking, urgent, quiet. I groaned as I tried to roll over onto my back and two of those shoes moved in my direction.

"God, AJ, don't move. We've got the paramedics coming. We'll get you to the hospital," Deputy Davis ordered.

"Travis? Did she kill Travis?" I couldn't breathe or see or think. *How could this happen twice in one lifetime?*

"Oh lord no, AJ. He's on his way...should be here any minute. When you didn't answer the phone, he called me. I got here as fast as I could with the damned flooding and trees down everywhere."

"Dora..." I started.

"She's dead. Gunshot wound to the chest. Big gun."

"Tell me about it. I've been staring at it all night. Why do little old ladies need to carry guns made for infantry use?"

He laughed. "I was talking about Barnes' gun. He had a 40 cal. Bigger than Dora's."

"Barnes?" I asked. "Where the hell did Barnes come from? I thought you were going to bring him in for questioning."

"FDLE said they asked him to come talk to us, maybe forced some kind of decision for him. He told the Lieutenant that he had some unfinished business to handle before he came by the office. But I have no idea how he ended up here unless he was tracking her. He was a decorated cop, very well respected. Maybe the cop in him wanted to stop her. No one will know for sure now." He sighed. "If she hadn't killed him, I wouldn't be surprised if we'd found him dead with his own gun."

Shane knelt beside me and covered me with a blanket from the sofa. "Where do you hurt?"

"Everywhere. I killed the fire, so it was dark. Then I charged at her for the gun, wanted to take it away. She was waiting to kill Travis. Then a man showed up and I thought it was Travis." My teeth were chattering, clicking like rollerblades on a tile floor.

"She was going to kill you, too. She and Barnes killed each other. You've got a hell of a gash, though. Looks like you hit the coffee table."

271

I heard a lot of commotion from the region of the kitchen. Davis pulled his gun and settled on his knees beside me. I closed my eyes. Too tired…

"AJ Buchanan you'd better be all right or I'm going to kill you," bellowed my husband. I laughed a little, but it hurt a lot.

I felt Davis move, and then Travis laid his head next to mine on the rug.

"You sound like me, Crimestopper," I whispered.

When I woke again, I was back in the Flagler Hospital emergency room in lovely St. Augustine. *Yet another visit through the Fast Track Department.*

"At this rate, maybe we'd better see if there's some sort of discount plan." I looked at Travis and tried to smile.

He sat beside me, my right hand clutched in his. "I'm sure none of our insurance policies will escape a hefty premium increase, that's for sure."

"My father. Is he all right?"

"Right as rain, honey. He'll be home tomorrow morning. I assured him you were fine, and he didn't need to rush back tonight."

A nurse maneuvered a stainless-steel rolling table around the curtain. A doctor followed behind her.

"We're going to suture your forehead, Mrs. Buchanan, then take a film, check for cranial injury. We'll have to x-ray that shoulder again, too."

"Do what you have to Doc, just do it fast. I want to go home."

\*\*\*

I was asleep in my own bed by three a.m. Sunday morning, snuggled against Travis. Since we'd entered the house by the front door, I assumed the back door had been boarded up for the time being.

It was almost noon on Sunday when I got myself together and headed downstairs where Travis, my father and Shane Davis were gathered in the living room.

Glancing in a mirror, I groaned. I sported dual black eyes, one of which was swollen shut, six stitches above my right brow and a dull pounding in my head. I figured lipstick wouldn't help, so I skipped it, going for the *au naturale* look.

"Good morning, gentlemen," I said. I sat next to Travis on the sofa. A gallon box of take-out coffee was on the table next to a box that smelled like fresh pastries from the Cafe.

"I'm afraid to ask how you are feeling, Antonia," my father said.

"I've felt better. Not recently, but I can remember a time. Of course, I've felt worse, too." I looked at Deputy Davis. "This is finally over, isn't it? If it's not, just lie to me."

273

"Everything but the mountain of required paperwork." He nodded. "I was just telling Travis that we have all we need to put this case to bed."

"Does Betty have to be involved?" I asked.

"Don't know," Davis said. "I suspect we can probably keep her out of most of it." He looked at the floor, then back at me. "She has a right to know what happened, though."

"I know. But the only one left to suffer will be Betty and none of this is her doing."

Travis patted my knee. "Maybe Betty doesn't need to know all the sordid details. But if she does, she's a big girl. We'll see her through it."

"Secrets are what started all this, might be time to break that cycle, I guess."

Davis nodded. "Everything documented becomes public record." He pointed at the journal that still lay on the hearth.

"Too bad that didn't make it into the fire, huh?" I should have burned Richard's tome first.

He shrugged. "Depends on what that is, I'd say. Couldn't be sure last night what needed to be tagged as evidence in your case what with all the blood and such. We tried to be respectful of your personal possessions."

With that, he got to his feet and shook hands with Travis and my father. I stayed seated since it was too much effort to move. I was eyeing up the box of pastries anyway.

"The State's Attorney will be in touch with you once they've gone through our reports. They'll need depositions and signatures. Hope you're feeling better real soon, AJ."

"Thanks for all you've done, Shane. Take care of yourself out there."

When he left, I snuggled back against Travis' chest, and he wrapped his arms around me.

"You have aged me twenty years, my love. Next time we get an evil email, we're going to the Grand Caymans. Your father can have Asta forward the mail."

"I told you, Yankee, Southern women don't run from trouble."

I felt him chuckle. "Then I'll shanghai you if you are going to be too stubborn for your own good. Life without you is not an option."

I laced my fingers through his and looked at our hands. I understood exactly how he felt.

\*\*\*

Betty called on Monday morning around nine with a promise to bring lunch when she came at noon. I explained that she'd need to use the front door as we were remodeling the kitchen doorway.

I had the fire going and was curled up on the sofa listening to a Robert Parker mystery on CD when she arrived.

I heard the rustle of plastic bags as she came through the porch door. Betty's laughter made me feel good and bad. She probably wouldn't be laughing when she left.

I shut off my CD player and pushed myself to my feet, reaching to take a bag from her loaded arms.

"What's for lunch?" I asked. Betty almost dropped the bucket of fried chicken when she saw my face. Travis saved the food with a graceful half-dive from across the room.

"Oh my gosh, not again, AJ. Please tell me you weren't hurt again on my behalf," she wailed.

"*This* time was on *my* behalf. The last time was on behalf of Margie Donovan."

"Sit down, please. You can fill me in while we eat lunch." We sat on either end of the sofa. Travis sat in the armchair by the fire.

Her father's journal lay in plain view on the coffee table, but she ignored it. Travis poured glasses of sweet tea, pulled the armchair across the room, and joined us.

"Shane Davis told me he called you about Dora," I started once our eating frenzy slowed to the occasional 'pick' here or there.

She sighed and tears filled her blue eyes. "He did. And I'm so sorry. It's very sad that I didn't know her better. Maybe some of this could have been prevented. Was it Dora who hurt you?"

Even a slight movement caused me to yelp, so I sat perfectly still. "You couldn't have done anything to change this, Betty. Dora was a tormented woman. And I don't think anyone saw the Barnes connection in time to figure this out, let alone stop it."

"She was quite mad, don't you think?" Betty pulled her jacket tighter around her.

"Did you know about her and your father?"

"I didn't know anything for sure, but Uncle Nate and mother often discussed Dora when they thought I wasn't listening. Her mental state was mentioned a time or two, but I didn't see it. I wasn't around her very much. She was a nurse. Someone who helped people, even if she wasn't very friendly toward mother. She would spend time in the study with Father, though. Now I understand that that was all about. Wonder if I was conceived on his desk?"

"Honey, don't do this to yourself," I said.

I motioned toward the thick book which had been relegated to the floor to make room for our lunch.

"Your father's journal actually contains entries by both your father and mother."

Betty's voice was soft, sad. "I thought I knew her, but she lied to me. Lies on top of lies. Matilda wasn't my real mother, at all."

I met her gaze. "She's the woman who loved you, who raised you, who did all she could to protect you."

"Do you really know who my birth mother is? For sure?"

I didn't answer her right away and she knew. "*Dora* was my mother?" The color drained out of her face so fast I was glad she was sitting down.

I nodded. "How much do you really want to know?"

"Was Nathan my father?"

"No, he loved you and Matilda very much, and Matilda loved him, but Richard Senior was your father."

"Well, if this isn't a classic bad redneck joke, I don't know what is."

"Dora was the child of your grandfather Joshua and his twin sister Sarah. Sarah died in childbirth, so Dora was raised by Matilda's mother, just as Matilda raised you."

"God, how sick this is. I sure am glad I didn't have any children. Who would want to pass on all these awful genes to another generation?" Her color was better, and she pulled her shoulders back.

"Is all this in that book, AJ?" she asked finally.

"Most of it. There were other papers for you too, but I had to burn them last night. Dora wanted it all destroyed."

Betty stared at me. "We should burn this, too. I get the creeps just looking at it."

"Up to you. You might change your mind later, though," I said. "If you destroy it now, it can't be replaced."

She pulled the book onto the table and ran her fingers over the gold-leaf letters. "That might be a good thing, but you've got a point, I suppose. Would you want to know all this if you were me?"

I risked a shrug. "I'm not a good one to ask, Betty. I'm still looking for the answers to why Rick is dead. Probably should let that go, but I don't seem to be able to do that. At least, not entirely."

Travis gathered up our left-over food and headed for the kitchen in silence.

Betty looked back at me. "I read enough of my father's other diary to know I don't want this. Let's burn it. Right now."

I nodded and we moved to the fireplace. I held the book while she tore out each page and placed it neatly on top of the logs. The fire crackled and we watched years of tragedy go up in smoke. Shakespeare would have been proud of the irony. So many deaths to protect secrets no one wanted to know.

"Travis," Betty called into the kitchen, "you and AJ need to take a vacation. Go someplace warm and quiet. Where you don't get set on fire, beat up, or shot at."

I burst out laughing. "He's been after me for weeks to do that. What do you think, honey? Ready to take that vacation?"

He winked from the doorway. "Sure, now that you can barely move a muscle, you're agreeable to a vacation. Well, I'm ready whenever you are. But what about the

Mayfield legacy? And Rick? And the starving children in Appalachia?"

I looked at Betty. "Although he's being a wiseass, he brings up a good point. Still want that local history done?"

"I'd like to do what my mother wanted, I meant that. When you get back from that vacation, you can capture the history in photographs. The people, the era, the loss of those things over time." She stared at the flames in the fireplace. "In black and white, I think."

I caught my husband's gaze and nodded. "That would make a good tribute, Betty. Because life is *anything* but black and white."

## About the Author

Born and raised in small-town New Jersey, Nancy was reading Carolyn Keene's mysteries by the time she was six. Once through that series, she embarked on adventures with Huck Finn, the Hardy Boys and the Bobbsey Twins. More than once she was in trouble for hiding in a tall maple tree to read instead of finishing her chores.

In 1999, she got the first "call." A short story was sold to a Virginia publisher, and she's sold short stories and articles regularly ever since, with the help of her long-time critique group.

She's the owner of On-Target Words, LLC, where she specializes in content editing, copy writing, and speaking to other writers about the craft skills she knows. Her website is http://OnTargetWords.com.

She lives in northeast Florida with her husband and an entertaining collection of felines.

She loves to hear from readers anytime, so be sure to drop her a line. Nancy@nlquatrano.com.

OTHER NOVELS BY N. L. QUATRANO
*Point and Shoot Series* from WC Publishing
STILL SHOT – Book 2. Winner of the Action and
Adventure Category in the international Book
Excellence Awards of 2019.

GONE IN A FLASH – Book 3 Fall, 2021.

*Amazing Grace Trucking Company Series* from Two
Stone Lions Press (with D. K. Ludas)

MERCIFUL BLESSINGS – Book 1. Award finalist in
the FAPA and FOREWORD INDIES contests, first
place RPLA winner.

KEEPING FAITH – Book 2. Apr. 2021

*SHORT STORIES BY NANCY L. QUATRANO*:

THE METHOD WRITERS w/a one of the Rogues
Gallery Writers

SNOWBIRD CHRISTMAS VOL 1 (2012)
A Christmas Collection of Short Stories

SNOWBIRD CHRISTMAS VOL 2 (2013)
A Christmas Collection of Short Stories

ONE AT A TIME by Caroline Wolff, as told to Nancy L. Quatrano

TELL THE CHILDREN by Caroline Wolff, as told to Nancy L. Quatrano

*Published as N. L. Quatrano*:
Mysteries:
CRIME SCENE NJ: Mystery by Garden State Authors, Volumes 1, 2, 3 (Out of print)

*Published as Nancy Quatrano*:
ROMANCE RECIPES FOR THE SOUL: An Inspiring Collection and Unique Real-Life Dating Stories
Frank Cabiroy, Pisces Press (1999)
*Coming Winter of 2015 by Nancy L. Quatrano*
(Short Story E-book)

YELLOW RIBBON, originally published by Wild Rose Press as YELLOW RIBBONS. This Writer's Digest finalist short story is dedicated to the men and women who serve our country in the military. Half of all proceeds will benefit the K9s for Warriors project in Northeast Florida.

Visit Nancy's author profile at Amazon Central:
https://amzn.to/3kIJ1Dq

www.ingramcontent.com/pod-product-compliance
Lightning Source LLC
Chambersburg PA
CBHW011441170626
46807CB00009B/3260